MANHATTAN
LOVE
SONG

MANHATTAN LOVE SONG

CORNELL WOOLRICH

With a new introduction by
Francis M. Nevins, Jr.

PEGASUS BOOKS
NEW YORK

MANHATTAN LOVE SONG

Pegasus Books LLC
45 Wall Street, Suite 1021
New York, NY 10005

First Pegasus Books edition 2006

Library of Congress Cataloging-in-Publication Data is available.

ISBN: 1-933648-07-4

Printed in the United States of America
Distributed by Consortium

Manhattan Love Song

Cornell Woolrich

Here is the story of a mad love, written against the mysterious
background of the underworld. Unlike the ordinary tale of this
type with its crude, realistic descriptions, this story is attuned in
style and pace to the exoticism that surrounds and controls the
life of Bernice.

MANHATTAN LOVE SONG: INTRODUCTION

Francis M. Nevins

Noir.

Any French dictionary will tell you that the word's primary meaning is black, dark or gloomy. But since the mid-1940s and when used with the nouns *roman* (novel) or *film,* the adjective has developed a specialized meaning, referring to the kind of bleak, disillusioned study in the poetry of terror that flourished in American mystery fiction during the 1930s and forties and in American crime movies during the forties and fifties. The hallmarks of the *noir* style are fear, guilt and loneliness, breakdown and despair, sexual obsession and social corruption, a sense that the world is controlled by malignant forces preying on us, a rejection of happy endings and a preference for resolutions heavy with doom, but always redeemed by a breathtakingly vivid poetry of word (if the work was a novel or story) or image (if it was a movie).

During the 1940s many American books of this sort were published in French translation in a long-running series called the *Série Noire,* and at the end of World War II, when French film enthusiasts were exposed for the first time to Hollywood's cinematic analogue of those books, they coined the term *film noir* as a phrase to describe the genre. What Americans of those years tended to dismiss as rather tawdry commercial entertainments the French saw as profound explorations of the heart of darkness, largely because *noir* was so intimately related to the themes of French existentialist writers like Jean-Paul Sartre and Albert Camus and because the bleak world of *noir* spoke to the despair that so many in Europe were experiencing after the nightmare years of war and occupation and genocide. By the early 1960s cinephiles in the United States had virtually made an American phrase out of *film noir* and had acclaimed this type of movie as one of the most fascinating genres to emerge from Hollywood. *Noir* directors—not only the giants, like Alfred Hitchcock (in certain moods) and Fritz Lang, but relative unknowns, like Edgar G. Ulmer, Jacques Tourneur, Robert Siodmak, Joseph H. Lewis, and Anthony Mann—were hailed as visual poets whose cinematic style made the bleakness of their films not only palatable but fantastically exciting.

Foster Hirsch's *The Dark Side of the Screen: Film Noir* (1981) and several other books on this genre have been published in the United States, and one can attend courses on *film noir* at any number of colleges. But there has not yet developed the same degree of interest in the doom-haunted novels and tales of suspense in which *film noir* had its roots. Although Raymond Chandler, the poet of big-city corruption, and James H. Cain, the chronicler of sexual obsession, have received the fame they deserve, the names of countless other *noir* writers are known mainly to specialists.

I have three names for one of those writers. He was the Poe of the twentieth century, the poet of its shadows, the Hitchcock of the written word. His name was Cornell Woolrich.

He was born in New York City on December 4, 1903, to parents whose marriage collapsed in his youth. Much of his childhood was spent in Mexico with his father, Genaro Hopley-Woolrich, a civil engineer. At age eight the experience of seeing a traveling French company perform Puccini's *Madama Butterfly* in Mexico City gave Woolrich a sudden sharp insight into color and drama and his first sense of tragedy. Three years later he understood fully that someday, like Cio-Cio-San, he too would have to die, and from then on he was haunted by a sense of doom that never left him: "I had that trapped feeling, like some sort of a poor insect that you've put inside a down-turned glass, and it tries to climb up the sides, and it can't, and it can't, and it can't."

During adolescence woolrich returned to Manhattan and lived in an opulent house on 113th Street with his mother and her socially prominent family. In 1921 he entered Columbia College, a short walk from home. He began writing fiction during an illness in his junior year and quit school soon afterward to pursue his dream of becoming another F. Scott Fitzgerald. His first novel, *Cover Charge* (1926), chronicled the lives and loves of the Jazz Age's gilded youth in the manner of his own and his whole generation's literary idol. This debut was followed by *Children of the Ritz* (1927), a frothy concoction about a spoiled heiress's marriage to her chauffeur, which won him a $10,000 prize contest and a contract from First National Pictures for the movie rights. Woolrich was invited to Hollywood to help with the adaptation and stayed on as a staff writer. Besides his movie chores and an occasional story or article for magazines like *College Humor* and *Smart Set*, he completed three more novels during these years. In December 1930 he entered a brief and inexplicable marriage with a producer's daughter—inexplicable because for several years he had been homosexual. After the wedding he continued his secret life, prowling the waterfront at night in search of partners, and after the inevitable breakup Woolrich fled back to Manhattan and his mother. The two of them traveled extensively in Europe during the early 1930s. His only novel of that period was *Manhattan Love Song* (1932), which anticipates the motifs of his later suspense fiction with its tale of a love-struck young couple cursed by a malignant fate that leaves one dead and the other desolate. But over the next two years he sold almost nothing and was soon deep in debt, reduced to sneaking into movie houses by the fire doors for his entertainment.

In 1934 Woolrich decided to abandon the "literary" world and concentrate on mystery-suspense fiction. He sold three stories to pulp magazines that year, ten more in 1935, and was soon an established professional whose name was a fixture on the covers of *Black Mask, Detective Fiction Weekly, Dime Detective,* and countless other pulps. For the next quarter century he lived with his mother in a succession of residential hotels, going out only when it was absolutely essential, trapped in a bizarre love-hate relationship that dominated his external world just as the inner world of his later fiction reflects in its tortured patterns the strangler grip in which his mother and his own inability to love a woman held him.

The more than one hundred stories and novelettes Woolrich sold to the pulps before the end of the thirties are richly var-ied in type and include quasi–police procedurals, rapid-action whizbangs, and encounters with the occult. But the best and best-known of them are the tales of pure edge-of-the-seat suspense, and even their titles reflect the bleakness and despair of their themes. "I Wouldn't Be in Your Shoes," "Speak to Me of Death," "All at Once, No Alice," "Dusk to Dawn," "Men Must Die," "If I Should Die before I Wake," "The Living Lie down with the Dead," "Charlie Won't Be Home Tonight," "You'll Never See Me Again"—these and dozens of other Woolrich suspense stories evoke with awesome power the desperation of those who walk the city's darkened streets and the terror that lurks at noonday in commonplace settings. In his hands even such cliched story lines as the race to save the innocent man from the electric chair and the amnesiac hunting his lost self resonate with human anguish. Woolrich's world is a feverish place where the prevail-ing emotions are loneliness and fear and the prevailing action a race against time and death. His most characteristic detective stories end with the discovery that no rational account of events is possible, and his suspense stories tend to close not with the dissipation of terror but with its omnipresence.

In 1940 Woolrich joined the migration of pulp mystery writers from lurid-covered magazines to hardcover books and, beginning with *The Bride Wore Black* (1940), launched his so-called *Black Series* of suspense novels—which appeared in France as part of the *Série Noire* and led the French to acclaim him as a master of bleak poetic vision. Much of his reputation still rests on those novels and on the other suspense classics originally published under his pseudonyms William Irish and George Hopley. Throughout the forties and fifties Woolrich's publishers issued numerous hardcover and paperback collections of his short stories. Many of his novels and tales were adapted into movies, including such fine *films noir* as Jacques Tourneur's *The Leopard Man* (1943), Robert Siodmak's *Phantom Lady* (1944), *Roy William* Neill's *Black Angel* (1946), Maxwell Shane's *Fear in the Night* (1947) and, most famous of all, Hitchcock's *Rear Window* (1954). Even more of Woolrich's work was turned into radio and later into television drama. He made a great deal of money from his novels and stories but lived a spartan and isolated life and never seemed to enjoy a moment of his time on earth. Seeing the world as he did, how could he?

The typical Woolrich settings are the seedy hotel, the cheap dance hall, the run-down movie house, and the precinct station back room. The dominant reality in his world, at least during the thirties, is the Depression, and Woolrich has no peers when it comes to putting us inside the life of a frightened little guy in a tiny apartment with no money, no job, a hungry wife and children, and anxiety consuming him like a cancer. If a Woolrich protagonist is in love, the beloved is likely to vanish in such a way that the protagonist not only can't find her but can't convince anyone she ever existed. Or, in another classic Woolrich situation, the protagonist comes to after a blackout—caused by amnesia, drugs, hypnosis, or whatever—and little by little becomes convinced that he committed a murder or other crime while out of himself. The police are rarely sympathetic, for they are the earthly counterparts of the malignant powers above, and their main function is to torment the helpless.

All we can do about this nightmare world is to create, if we can, a few islands of love and trust to sustain us and help us forget. But love dies, while the lovers go on living, and Woolrich is a master at portraying the corrosion of a relationship.

Although he often wrote about the horrors both love and love-lessness can inspire, there are very few irredeemably evil characters in his stories. For if one loves or needs love or is at the brink of destruction, Woolrich identifies with that person no matter how dark his or her dark side. Technically many of Woolrich's novels and stories are awful, but like the playwrights of the Absurd, Woolrich often uses a senseless tale to hold the mirror to a senseless universe. Some of his tales indeed end quite happily—usually thanks to outlandish coincidence—but there are no series characters in his work, and therefore the reader can never know in advance whether a particular Woolrich story will be light or dark, *allègre* or *noir;* whether a particular protagonist will end triumphant or dismembered. This is one of the reasons why so much of his work remains so hauntingly suspenseful.

Including *Manhattan Love Song.*

It was published in August 1932 by William Godwin, a small and unpretentious house with a reputation for what was then considered sexually frank material. It was read by few, reviewed almost nowhere, and swallowed up almost at once in the Sargasso Sea of forgotten books. Although packaged as mainstream fiction, by today's standards it's clearly a crime novel, with an exceptionally tight and unified structure and only three central characters, who are so well drawn that we come to see each of them as seen by himself or herself and also by each of the others.

The time is night, the year is 1928, the place is New York, and the opening paragraph is one that only Woolrich could have written:

> First she was just a figure moving toward me in the distance, among a great many others doing the same thing. A second later she was a girl. Then she became a pretty girl, exquisitely dressed. Next a responsive girl, whose eyes said "Are you lonely?," whose shadow of a smile said, "Then speak." And by that time we had reached and were almost passing one another. Our glances seemed to strike a spark between us in mid-air.

As if by a miracle, with not a hint of explanation, they know one another. There could be no other way. This is their destiny. Wade, the narrator, soon becomes a helpless slave to his passion for the enigmatically lovely Bernice. Under her spell he abandons his job, assaults and robs a homosexual actor to get money to spend on her, treats his wife Maxine, who still loves him desperately, like filth. And Bernice, who in some mysterious way is controlled by unseen powers in the city, responds so passionately to Wade's abject passion for her that she is ready to sacrifice everything she has and risk the powers' vengeance for the chance to start life over again with him. But as in so much of Woolrich's fiction, love opens the door to horror, and those who manage to survive have nothing left but to wait for the merciful release of death.

Woolrich's last pre–suspense novel firmly establishes the leitmotif of the love-struck couple cursed by an inexplicable malignant fate that leaves one dead and the other desolate. But *Manhattan Love Song* stresses the dark underside of the lovers' characters. Wade is a master of male chauvinism who verbally abuses his wife, throws hot coffee at her in his rages, closes out their pitiful savings account to finance his elopement with Bernice, and yet can be hauntingly tender with her on the brink of deserting her forever. Bernice calls her maid a "jig" (though she's no worse than the other characters when it comes to racism), torments the impoverished Wade by auctioning herself off at a sex party, refuses to tell him the nature of her entanglement with the unseen powers, but gradually becomes as helpless a victim of *amour fou* as Wade himself. It is an axiom in Woolrich that whoever loves or needs love is forgiven much.

Countless elements from Woolrich's later suspense fiction show up for the first time in concentrated form in *Manhattan Love Song*. The dialogue is studded with precisely the sort of whiny, mordant insults that the characters in his pulp stories of the later 1930s use for conversation. The insane force of love pulsates through every chapter, generating an intensity that keeps us from noticing the holes in the plot. Perhaps most

important, *Manhattan Love Song* is the earliest work of fiction
in which Woolrich used a first-person narrator, not to give us a
privileged viewpoint but to force us into a single consciousness
so that we are divided against ourselves, empathizing with the
character's torment and shuddering at his twisted soul.

The novel was never reprinted in Woolrich's lifetime and
has never appeared in paperback even more than a third of a
century after his death, but it meant so much to him that he res-
urrected elements from it several times during his later career.
In "Murder in Wax" (*Dime Detective,* March 1, 1935; collected
in *Darkness at Dawn,* 1985) he recycled the situation with
which *Manhattan Love Song* had reached its climax—a married
man is about to leave his wife for another woman, but she is
murdered just before they are to take off together, and he is
left to be convicted of the crime and sentenced to death—but
this time we see and feel the situation through the eyes of
the condemned man's abandoned wife, who narrates in first
person. In "Face Work" (*Black Mask,* October 1937; collected
as "One Night in New York" in *Six Nights of Mystery,* 1950)
we find another female narrator in pretty much the same situation. Stripper Jerry Wheeler, frantic to keep her kid brother
Chick out of the clutches of torch singer Ruby Rose Reading,
begs each of the lovers in turn to abandon their plan to go off
together to Chicago, but strikes out with both. That evening, a
few hours after Chick has left to pick up Ruby Rose at her
apartment, Jerry is visited by a tough police detective who tells
her that Ruby Rose has been strangled and Chick arrested for
her murder. After he's convicted and sentenced to die, Jerry desperately takes up a new identity as she races the executioner's
clock to prove that Ruby Rose's murderer was not Chick but
some other man in her life. That situation, augmented by countless emotional and psychological refinements, in turn became the
basis of one of Woolrich's most powerful pure suspense novels,
The Black Angel (1943).

Before he had written any of these variations on the theme,
the movie rights to *Manhattan Love Song* were bought by

Monogram, one of the sturdier of the many low-budget independent studios that came and went in the early years of talkies. The film, directed by Leonard Fields from a screenplay by Fields himself and David Silverstein, kept Woolrich's title but transformed his study in *noir* anguish into a tedious comedy about two wealthy sisters (Dixie Lee and Helen Flint) who lose all their money and turn over their mansion and their own services as housekeepers to the chauffeur and maid (Robert Armstrong and Nydia Westman) in lieu of back wages. Fields's "brutal direction and poor story adaptation," said *Variety,* "k.o. [the picture] for serious consideration." Thanks to its "elephantine pace," the reviewer continued, the film "wears itself out long before going anywhere." It's probably a mercy that all prints of the movie seem to have vanished.

Woolrich knew overwhelming financial and critical success, but his life remained a wretched mess, and when his mother died in 1957, he cracked. From then until his own death eleven years later he lived alone, his last year spent in a wheelchair after the amputation of a gangrenous leg, thin as a rail, white as a ghost, wracked by diabetes and alcoholism and self-contempt. But the best of his final "tales of love and despair" are still gifted with the magic touch that chills the heart. He died of a stroke on September 25, 1968, leaving no survivors. Only a tiny handful of people attended his funeral. His estate was left in trust to Columbia University, where his literary career had begun, to establish a scholarship fund for students of creative writing. The fund is named for Woolrich's mother. He left behind four unfinished books—two novels, a collection of short stories and a fragmentary autobiography—plus a list of titles for stories he'd never even begun. In one of these he captured the essence of his world and the world of *noir* in just six words.

First you dream, then you die.

In a fragment found among his papers after he was gone, Woolrich explained why he wrote as he did. "I was only trying to cheat death," he said. "I was only trying to surmount for a little while the darkness that all my life I surely knew was going to come rolling in on me some day and obliterate me." In the end, of course, he had to die, as we all do. But as long as there are readers to be haunted by the fruit of his life, by the way he took his wretched psychological environment and his sense of entrapment and loneliness and turned them into poetry of the shadows, the world Woolrich imagined lives.

CHAPTER ONE

First she was just a figure moving toward me in the distance, among a great many others doing the same thing. A second later she was a girl. Then she became a pretty girl, exquisitely dressed. Next a responsive girl, whose eyes said "Are you lonely?," whose shadow of a smile said, "Then speak." And by that time we had reached and were almost passing one another. Our glances seemed to strike a spark between us in midair.

I retraced my steps while she continued hers. It had been too sudden to be crude, or even noticeable at all. And I had raised my hat. You raise your hat when you meet some one. And I had met her, as any one could see. Not at all new under the sun, all that. But it was she and it was I. That made all the difference imaginable.

She was dressed almost entirely in blue, but her stockings were the color of a rifle-barrel glistening in the sunlight, and their texture was so thin that it merged into the pink of her skin, which showed through. She had eyes with sprites in them that came and went: little capering symbols of whimsicality and amusement, dancing figurines of mockery. And at times she drawled, "If you see what I mean," and a horrible expression that she had, "On the level?"

"Don't say that."

"Why not?"

"It's Third Avenue."

"Well?"

"You're—at any rate, Madison."

"That," she said, "is a thing I've never done before in all my life."

I smiled and asked her what that was.

"That, back there," she explained.

"You mean, meeting me this way?"

"Meeting any one this way. No, really—"

"Wade."

"No, really, Wade, I could tell by looking at you—"

It seemed absurd for her to think me nice. "You ought to know me!"

The street was gone now, and the lights of the street, and the taxis and the dangerous crossings, where one had to start forward and then shrink back, and stay close beside one another. We sat for a while somewhere along Seventh Avenue, and every so often a monstrous top set in the ceiling, all tin and bits of broken mirror, would begin spinning and throwing off a fine spray of drops of light that got in our eyes and rained down the walls like a new plague in a newer Egypt.

She extinguished her cigarette in the remains of the chop suey. "So much for that. To go back: Is there love at this table?"

Probably at every one of these tables, I told her, except perhaps the one at which the Cantonese cashier was sitting by himself. I already knew one could use a term like "Cantonese" in speaking to Bernice.

"Here, I'll put it this way. I don't feel love; now is there love at this table?"

"Half-love," I remarked. Said she, "I'd rather have a baked apple."

The whining music ebbed into the distance, the dancers melted away, the lanterns and the prismatic top faded from view, and in the tall, white apartment house Bernice said, "Put your hat down any place at all."

One knee was bent and her leg folded under her. Up and down the other, which touched the floor, coursed a mobile silvery gleam, oily as mercury. That was the electric light in the room, come to a head upon the silk that encased her calf. She alone could have lent grace and relaxation to so grotesque a posture.

The noises that came to us from the world outside were fewer now, but more distinct, meaning it had grown late. The lights were like planets now, ringed with luminous disks that were not there at all. To swallow was more stringent now, not as cool and grateful to the palate. I set a glass down, and the sound rang and then hummed in my ears for a long time afterward. This, like the halos about the lights, was not there at all, I realized.

"My birthstone," she said, showing me a ring. "I was born in May."

And then she looked at me more narrowly and did a strange thing. She took the ring off and dropped it on the inside of her dress.

"Once I had a ring," she explained, "and a friend. I lost them both at about the same time. If you see what I mean."

"Oh, I'd better scram," I told myself disconsolately. Only my feet wouldn't move.

"I'm going," I said.

"Well, go, then!" she answered.

But once I read about a flower that looks very harmless and sweet, yet when an insect comes near it, it suddenly folds around it and captures it; that's how it lives, by capturing the things that come too near it.

I took one of her hands and slowly disengaged it to hold it in mine. I studied it as though I had detached a part of her and the rest of her wasn't there any more. It was very soft, it was graceful, tapered and unlined, and ended in five little glazed ovals, like porcelain baked in an oven. It had, no doubt, stroked kittens, puppies, possibly a man or two. A lucky man or two. It had, no doubt, clasped playing cards in fan shape, road-sters' wheels, tall beaded glasses, and maybe even, in jest or white-faced deadliness, a purse-sized automatic revolver. How did I know, how could I tell? I pressed it to my lips, as though to assimilate at a stroke all its past experiences that I had had no share in. Then I grew weary and desperate with the kind of loneliness I had known so often and so well before now. The room, like a clumsy, improvised carousel, began to revolve about me, as though I were its pivot. For calliope it had my heart. Bernice shared in the general flux of everything I beheld. I was gazing up at her now from the floor.

"Loosen your collar," she murmured. "I'm a little afraid of you," she said. "You are the most perfect actor in New York, or else—I've met you eight years too late."

She laughed, as though in derision of some long-established value of her own which had just been set aside. "And I thought I knew them all! Oh, I was so sure at twelve o'clock that there was nothing could surprise me any longer and now, at three, I find myself back where I was eight years ago, believing that it *could* happen like this and *should* happen like this. That it should make the room reel around you and your knees play you false. Yes, that is what it should be; not clammy hands under tablecloths and laprobes, and checks in scaled envelopes handed to you by the colored doorman downstairs the morning after."

Her eyes sank to the level of mine as she dropped down beside me; our checks were pressed together now.

"The past is a lie. The past is something that no longer exists."

"Yes," she said docilely.

"And can you call a thing that no longer exists, true?"

"No."

"And has the past ever existed? Hasn't it always been just something in your mind?"

"Oh, no!" she contradicted. "For instance, eight years ago the past was still the *future*."

"You mustn't try to think like a man, that's one thing," I informed her sullenly. "Eight years ago the past was just as non-existent as today. There never *is* a past, don't you see?"

"Because you don't want there to be any. Oh, Wade, what blows you're letting yourself in for!"

"Did you ever know any one before you knew me? Did any one ever love you before I did? Then why aren't they here beside you, as I am?"

"The room would be filled with people," she breathed.

"Where are they?" I persisted. "How can you *prove* you knew them, *prove* they loved you, *prove* they really existed?"

"Oh, Wade," she cried piteously, "I can't! All I have to show for it is canceled checks!"

Rebelling, I kissed the past away from her lips. I kissed her eyes, and saw them droop. We were like two frantic, dying things, suffocating in a catastrophe of our own unchaining.

The sunlight, when at last I saw it, was diluted to the impotency of a pale lemonade washing over the floor and the walls. And the blur of sleep in my eyes made even this seem no more than a faraway gleam, imperfectly realized, like the flash of an oar far off at sea.

Beside me, she stirred and her eyes opened.

Her toe made a tiny pyramid of orchid taffeta for a moment. Then the pyramid sank from sight.

She bunched her shoulders and yawned. Then quickly covered her mouth with her hand, looked askance at me, and breathed, "Excuse me, I forgot you were here."

This took my breath away. My mouth dropped open.

"When I'm alone," she explained, "I can yawn all I want to. I forgot."

I looked around, but there was nothing to put over me except the fuming cataract of peach stuff she had affected toward the end of the night before. I put it around me, and incidentally made an armhole where there had been none before by the simple process of thrusting my hand in the wrong direction. I glanced covertly at her. She had not seen it happen. I left the room, and in the other room came face to face with a colored woman who was emptying cigarette-ashes with an air of extreme disinterest. She looked up and said "Good morning!" without an instant's hesitation, and even after I had seen her limpid eyes rest for a moment on the negligee I had around me like a toga, one bare arm hanging limply out, she did not smile, so self-controlled was she.

"Leave it outside the door when you go in," she said in the whisper of a fellow-conspirator. "I'll sew it up so she won't notice."

But this may have been simply policy on her part, this wish to conciliate every one, especially some one whom she had just seen for the first time.

Called Bernice all at once, in a voice that carried well: "Turn the warm water tap for me, Wade, and dump a lot of those pink crystals in."

The colored woman answered in gentle remonstrance, "I'm here, Miss Pascal."

"Let him do it," she ordered. "You can wash last night's glasses."

I at once adopted her own unmannerliness. "You can wait," I shouted hoarsely. "I'm in here now. And I don't suppose you have a razor?"

"Oh, order me about some more," she replied languidly. "It sounds so good. No, only a curved one for the arms. But there's a barber's shop downstairs in the building. I can call down for you and have them send some one up here."

"No, you better not do that, Miss Pascal," the colored woman interposed hastily. "It don't look right."

"Oh, but they know anyway," Bernice called back candidly.

"But that's a little bit too brazen," her mentor assured her.

I heard a startled gasp. "Well, I like that!" But nothing more was said about it.

At noon I extinguished my cigarette with a gesture (and a mental attitude to accompany it) of finality in the coffee dregs at the bottom of the cup, rose, and looked at her.

Once more, inevitably, she was different. She was lazy now, languid, plump. She was less intriguing, less desirable than she had been at any time since our meeting the evening before. She was moistening the tip of a finger with her tongue to remove a little imaginary sweet taste left by the brioche she had eaten a few minutes ago. When she got through with that finger, she went on to the next, and so on down the line, but fairly rapidly, so that the whole proceeding had an aspect of that insulting gesture made with the thumb to the nose. For a moment I even harbored a suspicion that this might be the case, but I noticed that her hand was pointed sidewise and not at me. The little rite concluded by her drying her fingers on a napkin and then tossing it down. "Good-bye," I said, "the whole dozen of you."

"Are there as many of me as all that?" she laughed, "Which aspect did you like best?" And then she looked at one of the pillows and hit it with her fist.

"Wrong again," was all I said.

She gave a toss of her head.

"For heaven's sake," I said irritably, "you were right about the calories last night. Look at those shoulders!" And I gave them a slight disdainful push. And then somehow I kissed her. And at once I was in love again, the reaction *away* from love was at an end, and she was lithe again and slim and all things attractive.

"And before I go," I said, crouching down with my hands on my knees so that our faces were on a level, "won't you tell me one thing? Who is he?"

"Who is who?" she said. "What are you talking about?"

"I know you don't make hats or take in washing."

"No," she said, "only stupid people do. But then, also, only stupid people are ever completely happy."

"I've been stupid," I assured her, "ever since nine last night."

Her cigarette quivered between her lips as she spoke. "What a swell set of sides you've had handed you. What's the name of the show going to be?"

"Good-bye," I said, straightening up.

"Can you find your way out all right?"

"It's all right about my finding my way out. The thing is, can I find my way in again?"

"Well, can you? I don't hand out road maps."

"You're the boss," I informed her philosophically.

"Suppose," she said, pinching her lower lip meditatively, "you take this number here—" And she struck the base of the little cream-colored telephone with her thumbnail, "but first you've got to promise something. Don't ever stay on if any one's voice but mine answers. Get right off without saying a word. Will you do that? Don't ask for me, and don't even say hello. Now, you know my voice, and Tenacity isn't here in the evenings. The jig," she explained Tenacity. "So it's really quite simple."

I started to whistle the minute I had shut the door behind me. To be in love, why, it was swell!

CHAPTER TWO

I looked back and her house was gone, sunken, swallowed up in the masonry quicksand of New York. I sank into it myself a moment later, plunging into an iron hut with a ground-glass roof that stood on the sidewalk, down a flight of cement steps laved by tepid air, onto a concrete platform flooded with tawdry dusty electric light. A roar, a hiss, a current of wild air carrying leaves of newspaper on its bosom, and the opposite platform had vanished behind a long row of dirty lighted windows and pneumatic doors that slipped effortlessly back like secret panels in a detective story. But when they attempted to close again, there was always some latecomer, now at one car, now at the other, to squeeze himself in at the last moment with a sheepish grin of satisfaction, until at last a guard came and glowered and pulled each one definitely shut with a swing of his arm.

I saw that there were seats, but I was so used to standing that I stood anyway, my wrist linked around a porcelain hoop. I felt more comfortable standing. I was one of that vanishing race who, when they had a seat, relinquished it to the first woman who entered, unless they were too stout or smelled of garlic. This was an express, hence all the locals going in the same direction passed it with quick facility. Laboriously it overtook them at the in-between stations, only to be passed again a moment or two later. The idea seemingly being that, since an express was an express, it could rest on its laurels.

Up the steps again, the fresh air meeting me halfway and seeming to say, "Hello, you back again?" A shower of sunlight, the legs of passersby, then suddenly the whole city was in focus again. Oh, I don't mean I thought of all these things; they simply passed through my mind without my mind doing any work at all.

Bernice's image had gone hurrying away on the train I had just left. Another took its place, bringing with it discomfort, diffidence, and the dregs of yesterday's cold resentment. I put my key in the door and turned the lock, but after the bolt was gone and the knob free, I still didn't turn it for a moment but stood there with my head bent, listening or thinking. Evidently thinking, for there was nothing to listen to. "Tail between your legs, as if you were whipped," something inside me commented, and I reared away from the thought, went in, and shut the door forcibly behind me. At the same time a chair creaked. I put my hat on the little three-legged table and stood leaning negligently against the open doorway next to it, looking into the room beyond, one hand in my hip pocket.

Now the image that had taken the place of Bernice's swiftly left my mind, rushed into the room beyond and presented itself to me in the flesh, dressed in a sleeveless house frock with a little rubberized apron over it. No peach negligees here. Little cracked patent-leather pumps, each with a childish strap over the instep, side by side on the floor, immovable in angry determination. Within them were the same small graceful feet that had danced with me eight years ago to the strains of *The Japanese Sandman,* that I had kissed many times in fervor, and once, much later, trodden on brutally with my whole weight, to make her cry out, to show her who was master and that she must not throw things at me, especially hot coffee.

At sight of me, Maxine became galvanized into action. She flashed out of the chair as suddenly as though a spring had been released under her, letting it rock unheeded behind her, and started out of the room in the opposite direction, toward the bedroom. It occurred to me that, womanlike, she had timed the whole thing wrongly. That first creak of the chair, while I was still at the door, had told me she had heard me. She should have quitted the room then, if she was going to. But no, she had to wait and make sure that I would *see* her get up and leave the room, to drive the point home more forcibly. If it had been a man, and the sight of any one was as intolerable to him as she

pretended the sight of me was to her, he would have gotten up
in the first place, and not waited to do the whole thing under
observation.

"Now, listen—" I remonstrated.

"Don't talk to me," she said, but inconsistently remained
in the room and turned to me to do some talking on her own
part. "So you finally decided it was time to come back, did
you? Probably because you were hungry or needed a shave or
something."

"There's where you're wrong," I laughed grimly, "I passed a
million barber shops on my way here."

"I suppose you think I should feel flattered that you came
back at all. Well, I got along beautifully without you, it was so
peaceful and quiet!"

"Sure it was," I said, "with all the neighbors' radios going
at the same time."

"You try that again," she went on, "and you won't find me
here when you get back!"

I finally took my shoulder away from the door and came into
the room. I sank into a chair and put a match to a cigarette. "What
are you trying to do?" I said. "Start all over again? Didn't we have
enough yesterday?"

"You think all you have to do," she assured me, "everytime
anything comes up, is walk out the door and that ends it. Then
you can come back when you please and everything'll be
peaches and cream."

She was crying meanwhile.

"You don't act the least bit sorry. And oh, Wade, the awful
things you said! They haunted me all night."

Outside the window a radio started to play *Kiss and Make
Up*. She drooped toward me until our foreheads touched. I closed
my eyes, thought hard of Bernice, and kissed her devoutly. But
she must have noticed something, because she remarked half-
laughingly, but with an undertone of injury, "It's just like taking
medicine, isn't it?"

I told her it wasn't at all. "How do you get that way?"

Lord knows, it shouldn't have been. I watched her as she stood by the window looking out, holding the green net curtain pinned to the frame with one hand. She was young, younger than I was, undoubtedly younger than Bernice was. She was slim-waisted. We had decided not to have children. I didn't want them around. She had never had any, so didn't know what it would be like and consequently didn't miss them. Hence her figure and her face were just what they were the night I first looked at her. But I had looked at that face daily now for several thousand days. I mean, even Cleopatra would have palled on one in less time than that. And furthermore, Maxine had never outgrown the fads and foibles of the season I met her. It was as though she had crystallized immediately after marrying me. She still wore the lumpy, chopped-off, bobbed hair of 1920. She still put rouge on in two round fever sores when she went out. Though I hadn't danced with her in a long time, I suspected her of still shaking her whole body in your arms. The jazz age had been deplorable enough, as I remembered it, but to have to live with a leftover from it was asking too much. Good looking or otherwise.

"You'll never know," she said, still at the window, "just what I went through last night and this morning."

"We've got to cut out this animal-baiting, both of us," I suggested dully.

"It's funny about a man," she went on, as though talking to herself. "In the beginning, they do all the running after you, they can't let you alone, can't live without you. And then just as soon as you begin to see things their way, and tell yourself, 'Yes, he was right, I can't live without him either,' they seem to have gotten over it. When anything comes up, *you* walk out that door with a bang, and I know what you're thinking just as though I were inside your head. You're thinking: 'I've had enough of her for a while! I'm not going to think about her again until I'm good and ready to come back.' But I sit here thinking about nothing else but you the whole time you're gone. It's funny, that's all."

"Well, I'm here now," I said with an inward sigh, "so come on over, and if you still want to cry some more, I'll mop up after you; and if you want to smile, why, I'll smile right back at you."

She didn't cry any more, but she didn't smile much either; she seemed to be contented just as she was, in my arms. I thought, "Good Lord! what am I going to do with this kid? I wish she'd fall in love with someone else all at once." I stroked the top of her head and pressed my check to it, and touched the tip of her ear, where she had a little pendant of violet glass attached, and lifted it with my finger and let it drop again, the stupid ornament.

I was too sensible to wish I'd never met her and never married her, because our love had been beautiful while it lasted, but all my life I've hated responsibility, and what worse responsibility was there than this: to have her keep right on loving me after I had stopped loving her (except as a reflex action).

"And I sat there until two o'clock," she was saying, "and the light got so it burned my eyes, so I put it out and kept right on sitting there in the dark. And I thought any moment the phone would ring, I said to myself, 'I *can't* go to bed like this, without hearing from him. My Wade never did this to me before.' But the phone just *wouldn't* ring. I got up one time and took it in my hand and shook it, and *still* it kept quiet. Then after a while it got so I didn't care very much any more, the worst was over, and I couldn't've felt any more rotten than I did. *You* understand, don't you, honey? I just couldn't keep on wanting anything as much as all that. It was taking everything I had. Then I closed my eyes a second, and all of a sudden it was broad daylight and the dumbwaiter buzzed for the garbage. I felt like going down on it with the rest of the cast-off junk. That's when I did most of my heavy crying, when the sun started to come in the kitchenette window and I smelt bacon broiling and heard the lady over us say, 'Get up, Sam, your coffee's ready.' Gosh, it would've been sweet to see your morning grouch just then, and hear you say, 'Where the hell are the towels?' and 'Jesus, how I hate this place!' and all the things you always say! I even envied the morning you threw the cup of coffee at me, because I had you with me then, even if my chest did get scalded."

I was getting alarmed at all this. I covered her mouth with my hand. I didn't want to hear all about how much she loved me. If she couldn't tell me she was starting to grow indifferent, like I was, at least she could keep still. "That isn't love, Maxie, that's—that's almost hypnotism. You want to cut it out, I don't like to hear you talk like that. You make too much of me" ("and make it tough for me," I added to myself.)

We sat down to eat. Maxine had the table lowered from the wall and covered with orange and green dishes that came from Japan via the five-and-ten. We had canned tomato soup, canned spaghetti, canned pineapple, and evaporated milk. The bread was not canned, but it came wrapped by machinery in wax paper and already sliced. "Awfully thoughtless of them," I remarked sociably, "to make us go to all the trouble of buttering it ourselves. Us pioneers certainly endure hardships."

"Well," she observed, passing between the gas range and the table a number of times, "the little there was to do, I did it. You're idea of chipping in is to get yourself smelling like a barbershop."

And over our heads, at the same time, we heard a chair indignantly clamped down, and the lady upstairs remarked in high dudgeon to her spouse: "Oh, *yeah?* Well, don't eat it then, if you're so particular! Too bad about you!"

"Find out what it is," I suggested. "If he doesn't want it, maybe we could use it down here."

"What's the matter with you, Wade?" Maxine remonstrated. "You're crazy!"

"Do you dare me?" I insisted.

We listened a moment longer. "Believe me, I've got something better to do than slave over a hot stove all day for you. Shut up!" This last explosive admonition would have been audible even in a much better-built house than ours was. I thought: "It'll be a feather in her cap; she won't refuse," and prided myself on my knowledge of feminine psychology.

"Do you know her?" I asked Maxine eagerly.

"No," she said, "and this is no time to be interrupting them. You'll get yourself disliked. Come back here."

I went to the dumbwaiter shaft, opened the panel, and called up: "D-twelve! Oh, D-twelve!"

The panel above me opened and a man's voice growled, "Who is it?"

"The floor below," I answered cheerfully. "Couldn't help overhearing your Mrs. just now. Listen, sport, how about sending down a little dish of that stuff, whatever it is? We don't get much home cooking down here."

I heard Maxine's wail from the depths of the kitchenette. "Oh, Wade, you're terrible! You don't know how mortified I am."

The gentleman I was conversing with replied truculently, "Think you're wise, don't you? Why don't you learn to mind your own business!" And the panel slammed back. I waited. A second later it opened again and a persuasive feminine voice queried: "Hello? Hello below?"

I reached behind me, seized the eavesdropping Maxine by the elbow and dragged her forward, changing places with her.

"Yes," she said embarrassedly, "my husband got a notion he would like to try somebody else's cooking for a change. You know how men are. The grass is always greener in the other fellow's yard." She laughed apologetically. "Oh, that's awfully nice of you. I'm Mrs. Wade. Thank you so much, Mrs. Greenbaum." This went on for quite some time. They seemed to be exchanging recipes.

"Here," she said, coming away from the dumbwaiter at last with a platter in her hand, "you nut! Here's some lovely tapioca pudding for you."

"Oh, God!" I said, sinking weakly back in my chair and covering my eyes with one hand, "and I thought it was a steak!"

"Now," she said, "I hope you're satisfied. As a result of this, I'll probably have to say hello to her every time I meet her going up in the elevator. Or else sit here and entertain her all afternoon when you're away. Phone the movie house and find out what's going on."

I felt like saying, "It's polite to wait till you're asked."

I thought the picture would never be over. I squirmed and gritted my teeth in the baleful silverish glow that went on and on. I thought, "It's not *they* who should be paid a couple of grand a week for making faces, it's *we* who ought to be paid for sitting and watching." Then we were back again, and Maxine snapped on the lights, while I put the milk bottle outside the door and locked the apartment for the night. Another day was over. But what good was that, when the one after would be just like it?

I delayed as long as I could, after she had gone to bed and even after she had turned out the bed light. I stalked around in the living room with my coat off and my tie loosened. There wasn't going to be any making up of the row of the night before. I mean, we were made up already, but there weren't going to be any tokens of it. But there wasn't anything to read (and I hated reading, anyway) and there wasn't anything to do. I went into the kitchenette, and there was that awful tapioca pudding of Mrs. Greenbaum's staring me in the face. I emptied it into the sink and came out again. I pulled up the shades and looked out of the window. The sky was all brick dust, and there was no moon. Suddenly, standing there like that, I realized I had been praying, I had been saying, "Oh, Lord, give me a break. Let something romantic, something exciting, happen to me. Only once, if never again. Before I'm too old. Break up this life of mine. Never mind about mending it again, I can do that myself. Why did I ever marry her? Without her, every minute would have been an adventure! It isn't fair—"

I went inside, jumped out of my things, and got into my own bed. She may have been awake or she may have been asleep, it didn't matter to me.

Noise woke me up, great rolling drumbeats of it. I opened my dazed eyes, and outside the windows it would be all black one minute and all platinum the next, with a great big crash. And in that minute rain began to hiss down, and the curtains did a dance of the seven veils. "Quick, close the windows,

Wade!" Maxine whimpered, and one of the tinsel flashes showed her to me in the next bed, with her arm flung before her face and the pillow over her head instead of under it.

"What's the matter, scared?" I laughed, and got up and pulled down the sashes. That robbed the storm of all its dignity, made it just a stage effect in an old-fashioned melodrama, with the room very quiet all of a sudden and the flashes removed to a distance and not much better than an electric sign with the current flickering and dying down.

"I'm *still* scared," she informed me in a certain tone.

"Have a cigarette," I said. "I'm going back to sleep."

Presently she said, "I have a cigarette, but I haven't got a match."

I took a folder of them from under my pillow and passed them to her across the aisle between the two beds. In grasping them, she reached too far up on my arm. I could feel her fingers slip almost up to my elbow. I left the matches and took the arm away.

In the morning I was dreaming of Bernice. I was saying, "There's nothing worse than an earthquake; stand close to me in the doorway here until it passes," when Maxine woke me by shaking my shoulder.

"My goodness," she said, "I don't know where you were the night before last, but you certainly act as though you're making up for lost sleep. Come on, the coffee'll get cold."

"Where's a towel?" I grumbled, with my eyes still shut.

"Now don't start that," she said. "I laid one out for you."

I got up, leaned sleepily against the wall for a minute, then went out, jumped under the cold water, and began hitting myself from all directions. It was only when I was all through that I realized I had forgotten to take my pajamas off. They were clinging around me like wet elastic. So I knew by that what kind of a morning it was going to be. I felt sorry for her for a moment, and wondered if it wouldn't be kinder and more advisable to walk straight out as soon as I was dressed and swallow a glass of orange juice at the corner drug store instead of raising hell for the next half-hour. But she wouldn't have understood if I had, and what's the use of being self-sacrificing when the motive isn't made clear to the bystander?

But when I was dressed and went in and sat down, I kept the fingers of my right hand crossed.

She laughed charmingly, poor Maxine. "It's cleared up beautifully," she said. "I was terribly scared when we were having that storm last night."

"I know," I said briefly.

"Well, you didn't do much about it," she went on good-naturedly.

"What did you expect me to do, lay a hot-water bottle at your feet?"

"Well, you don't have to look so awful, Wade."

"Well, don't look at me, then."

She got off the subject in a hurry. "The lightning turned the milk sour. We'll have to use some of the evap., I'm afraid."

"I knew that was coming," I said.

"Why, you must be a mind reader," she suggested gently.

I thought, "It's a good thing *you're* not. If you could read mine right now, you'd dive under the bed in a hurry."

"Lousy," I said in reference to the coffee.

"It would be," she sighed, "no matter what was in it. If I hadn't told you, you wouldn't know the difference."

I enlarged on the subject.

"Well, don't take it, then," she said indifferently. "You don't have to, you know. Nobody's going to make you."

"Yeah!" I barked, "and I'm going to feel swell by the time I get to Forty-Second Street, you didn't stop to think of that, did you?"

"Oh," she moaned, "what am I going to do with this man?" And glanced entreatingly at the clock.

"Don't worry, affectionate, I'm going," I laughed grimly. And I looked down at the coffee cup for a second.

She saw me and forestalled me. She had learned by experience what I was thinking. She quickly took it off the table and emptied it down the sink. "No matter what happens to me now," she said, "at least it won't be another scalding."

That turned the trick, somehow. She probably expected it to as little as I did myself, but nevertheless it did. I laughed, went over to her, put my arms around her, and pressed my face against hers. "You poor kid," I droned, "why don't you go out and get yourself a pair of brass knuckles one of these times and rearrange my front teeth?"

"I'm just a dumb frail, like you say when you're drunk," she said. "I wouldn't hurt a tooth in your head. It's funny," she added thoughtfully, "in this life, one of us always has to do the bossing. Upstairs it's Mrs. Greenbaum, to judge by the sounds we hear, but in this family it's *you.*"

"Since when?" I said. "It's news to *me.* I'm afraid you're taking me for a sleigh ride."

She came to the door with me, and then when I got down to the street she came to the window to say good-bye some more. I didn't bother looking up, so she tapped on the pane. When I turned my head, she threw up the sash and leaned out to call down that old one of eight years ago. "Don't take any wooden nickels."

"Sure I will," I answered, "so I can pass 'em on to you." And waved, and went away.

For a little while everything was all right. I even stepped up on a high rickety chair under an awning to have my shoes shined. All my life, that, and a haircut, and a shower, have been barometers of well-being to me. Then my newly glistening shoes, gleaming like burnished bronze, carried me down into that twilight grotto they call the subway. The turnstiles made a continual popping sound, like machine-gun fire in that faraway war I so blissfully missed. Then a red comet and a green one, side by side, came hurtling out of the gloom, and behind them, like an accordion, a long row of lighted cars expanded and came to a standstill. I took my place before a seated lady with a little boy on her lap, tilted my chin, and stared down my nose at a gaudy placard showing a girl with what looked like a strip of gelatine pasted over her mouth. The little boy started to wipe the soles of his shoes on my trousers. The lady noticed it and said indulgently, "Put your feet down, Stefan." "Or else put your hands up," I thought, "and fight like a man," and moved away from there.

Then it was five o'clock and I was still standing in the crowded car aisle, only now the train was going in the opposite direction. And the luster had been trodden from my shoes and I had about sixty kilowatts less energy, that was all. I got out finally and pulled my clothing after me. Luckily, it still stayed on. Going up the steps, still in a crowd, the man in front of me missed a step and went down on his knees. I picked up his hat for him. A girl on the other side of him picked up the halibut steak he was bringing home to his wife. I could tell it was halibut steak by the smell. And the impact against the steel-rimmed step didn't help it any, either. "Maybe," I said to myself unfriendly, "that's some of *your* business too. Are *you* going to eat it?"

She wasn't in when I got there. There I was, back where I had started from. "Now, what the hell did I get out of that?" I thought morosely. "Just so they won't cut off the gas and electricity on us at the end of the month!" I picked the gin bottle up from the floor of the broom closet, poured two inches into a glass, went in and took a shower. One that could be heard out on the street, I'm sure. I thought I heard the doorbell ring, but wasn't sure. But when I was through toweling and had my shirt on, I went out to see, and Maxine had come in. She had deposited a big brown-paper bag full of stuff on the kitchen table and was sitting on a chair alongside of it, elbow on the table, holding her head in her hand. She lifted it to remark, "You couldn't even let me in, could you? I stood out there ringing away for fully five minutes, doing a juggling act with this stuff in one hand and my key in the other!"

"How was I going to open the door?" I said. "I was all wet."

"What was that?" I thought I had heard her say, "You always are." "Anyway," I went on, "you believe in giving delivery boys a swell break, don't you? What are they getting paid for?"

"Oh, don't bother me," she groaned. "I'm too tired to answer any deep questions right now."

I turned to leave the room; at the door, though, I turned a second time to answer this, hands in my back pockets. I evidently felt it needed answering. "Tired from *what?*" I sneered, "sitting around on your fanny all day? That's about all you do, as far as I can make out." Which, I figured, should have held her for awhile. Expecting me to answer doorbells in the nude! Even if she was my wife, there might be other people using the hallway at the same time.

"That's consideration!" she said. "How do *you* know what I'm doing? Television hasn't come in yet, has it?" She walked very close to me, and there wasn't much friendship in our glance. "So you think I'm sitting around all day doing nothing. Who do you think washes up the dishes after you've gone?"

"What's there to that?" I assured her. "Park 'em in the sink, turn on the water, and let evaporation do the rest—"

"Who do you think keeps the place clean, the Board of Health?"

"Maybe that's why I find our four-legged friends in the bathtub every now and again."

"Who do you think sends out the laundry? Who do you think makes the beds? Who do you think—"

"Oh, keep your funnies," I said. "I'm not end man in a minstrel show."

She was still standing close to me. It got on my nerves. "Don't crowd," I said, and gave her a push.

"Yes," she said, "that's what you're best at!"

"As long as I'm good for something, that's a help."

"Well," she cried, pointing rapidly at this and that, "there're the chops and there's the stove and there's the table—so if you want to eat, go to it! I'm going in and have a good cry. You can go to hell."

"I'll stop off at a restaurant on my way," I called after her. "I'm not pansy enough to get a kick out of doing *your* work for you!" And picked up my hat and went.

And sitting in state at a table in the "Original Joe's Restaurant" with a veal stew in front of me, I addressed the image in my mind in this wise: "And I don't have to have *you,* either. I can get along without any one. I can get along by myself." The image was Bernice's, not Maxine's. But with the dessert before me, I suddenly stood up and walked into a phone booth, dropping my napkin midway on the floor, where it lay like a challenge.

I pulled the glass slide after me, a light went on, and I got out my little book. "Tha-a-at's right," I assured the operator. It started to ring at the other end. It kept on ringing at the other end. I changed the foot I was standing on. Then I changed back again. I was so nervous I felt like going to the men's room. Wouldn't it ever stop ringing at the other end? Fourteen, fifteen, sixteen, seven—. Suddenly the operator got on again. "Your party hasn't answered yet." As though I didn't know that! "Shall I keep on ringing?"

"Do that little thing," I said, "if it takes all night." Meantime the dessert out there was getting warm and the coffee getting cold. No one had picked up the napkin yet, either.

And *still* it rang. "The dirty stay-out!" I commented. I started to work the little hook up and down to get the operator back. I wanted my nickel back. I had given up hope, you see. And suddenly the ringing stopped and there was a faint click at the other end. The receiver had been lifted. But there wasn't a sound. Whoever it was was waiting to hear my voice first. And she had told me not to open my mouth, not even to say hello, unless I heard her voice first. So a new kind of endurance contest began then and there. But I wasn't good at it, I had too much at stake. I gave in. "Hello?" I said formally.

"Hello?" a man's voice answered. "Who do you want?"

I couldn't've gotten off the line if I had wanted to. "Miss Pascal there?" I said mildly.

"Who're you?" was the immediate result of this.

"Is she or isn't she?"

"You a friend of hers?"

I knew I'd never get past him to her even if she *was* there, and why make it tough for her? There was always another day.

"I'm the repair man," I said, "for the City Service Radio Corporation. We've had a call from her saying her instrument needed looking over."

"Seven in the evening," he told me, "is a peculiar time to be going around repairing radios."

"The slip I have here is marked 'Urgent,'" I answered, "and we guarantee our customers day and night service, so I called to find out if it was all right for me to come up."

"The closest you'll get to here," he assured me, "is where you are now."

"It's up to you," I said philosophically. "If you prefer static to good reception, we ain't gonna cry about it."

"And thank the City Service Radio Corporation for me," he remarked emphatically. "It's darn sweet of them, considering I got the instrument at Landay's."

"Y' dirty punk!" I exploded, and hung up.

So you see the call wasn't exactly a success.

I went back to my table and started to think it over. The bisque tortoni was just whey by now, anyway. I told myself I might've known it would go wrong, I should have waited until some other night. I went over the conversation word by word, and the more I went over it, the more something struck me. About his voice. Especially in the opening phrases. He had sounded more scared than I was. As though he had no right to be where he was, and as though he were afraid of being caught there. "But still, if he bought the radio," I reminded myself, "he has every right to be there." There was no getting around *that*. And yet he hadn't seemed at all at home, at all at ease.

Just as I stuck my hand in my pocket to get out some money to pay for my dinner, a bell rang, and then a waiter came over to me and asked if I had just put in a call from the middle booth.

"One of 'em, anyway," I answered. "Yeah, I think it was the middle one, the stuffiest of the lot."

"Well, they're calling back," he said. "You're wanted on the line."

"Who they asking for?" I said cautiously, noting my hat within grasping distance.

"All they said was 'The party that just got off this wire.' The cashier told me it was you."

I knew how it had happened: whoever hangs up first on a telephone makes it possible for the other party to trace the call through the operator. In the intrigue racket it's a good rule to always let the other fellow hang up first, if you don't want your whereabouts known. He had evidently stayed on after I did, and found out it was a restaurant. I thought I'd go back and give him hell.

But when I got in the booth and picked up the loose receiver, it was Bernice herself.

"Hello," she said immediately, "is this the manager of the City Service Radio Store?"

"No," I said, "it's Wade."

"Well, I'd like an explanation," she went on, as though she hadn't heard me. "Some one just rang my apartment claiming to be a repair man for your concern. And used insulting language—"

"Who was he, honey?" I said softly, "the big stiff that answered the first time?"

"Now, I not only never sent you people any calls, but my radio didn't come from you in the first place. I want that distinctly understood—"

"Keep on talking," I said. "Gee, your voice is beautiful!"

"If I'm annoyed like this again," she threatened, "I'll notify the police. It's very embarrassing, to say the least."

"Have you missed me?" I crooned. "Have you been thinking about me like I've been thinking about you?"

She went on improvising beautifully. "Oh, he was drunk? Well, he certainly acted it, my dear man. And I'm surprised at your firm for employing people like that. Now, would you mind telling me just how he got hold of my telephone number and my name?"

"Baby," I agreed, "that's going to be a hard one for you to answer."

But she had ideas of her own. "I beg your pardon, I am *not* listed," she contradicted.

"When am I going to see you again? When are you going to give me a break? Tomorrow night? Wednesday night?"

"Oh, he was formerly employed by Landay's and has a list of their customers? So that's it! That explains it."

"How about tomorrow night?" I pleaded. "Just say yes or no, can't you?"

"No," she said, and went on, "I don't want you to discharge him. I'd be afraid he'd hold a grudge against me. Especially if he drinks."

"The night after, then?" I said. "How about that?"

"Yes," she said, "please see that it doesn't happen again."

"You swell thing!" I gasped.

"Thank you," she said briskly. "Good-bye!"

I was mopping my forehead when I came out, the bulb had heated the booth until it felt like an incubator, but I was happy, all right. I even went back to my table and almost left the waiter a fifty-cent tip. Almost, but not quite. I changed it to a thirty-five-cent one at the last moment. If a man has no more ambition than to be a waiter, why encourage him by letting him think there's money in the game?

So I left that little restaurant I'd never been in before and never went to afterward, like so many other places I've only gone to once in life. But afterward, whenever I heard the word "restaurant," my mind saw that one place and not any of the others, saw the phone booth lighted from within and the napkin lying on the floor and the glass case full of cigar boxes with a cash register sitting on top of it.

Then immediately afterward, it seemed as though I had hardly stepped out of the door, I was in another phone booth and it was Wednesday.

"This is me, honey," I said.

"Well, Wade," she said, "I don't know what to say to you. I'm going out."

Forty-eight hours' anticipation went smash. "You told me you'd be in tonight," I answered. "What kind of a chiseler are you!"

"Don't get fresh, Wade," she suggested docilely. "It isn't going to get you anywhere."

"It's going to get me where I want to be," I told her, "and that's with you."

"I doubt it," she said.

I gave my necktie a tug. "If you don't want to see me, well—"

"I didn't say that I don't want to see you. I said I'm going out. This came up all of a sudden, and—there it is."

"Business before pleasure," I said poisonously.

"I'll hang up if you say anything like that to me again," she threatened.

I waited a moment to see if she would, afraid that she would, but she didn't.

"When do you expect to get back?" I said finally.

"I may get back at twelve—and I may get back at dawn. Why?"

"Make it twelve. Leave the key with the doorman, and I'll wait up for you. What's your favorite flavor sandwich? I'll bring some in with me."

"Just a *minute!*" she protested. "Not so fast. How do you think that's going to look?"

"Swell to me."

"Yes, but to the doorman?"

"I'll tell him I'm your big brother."

"You'd better think up a better one than that," she said sharply. "This isn't 1910."

"Well, how about it, lovable?"

"Wade, I'd like to see you awfully," she assured me, "but I'm afraid—suppose someone insists on seeing me home?"

I knew that was what was really troubling her, not the doorman at all. She probably had him well fixed. "Oh," I said negligently, "if any one does, tell him you're having the place repapered, tell him anything, lose him in the lobby. You're probably good at that, anyhow."

"Well—" she said.

"If you don't leave the key," I said, "I'm going to wait for you downstairs anyway, so take your choice."

"Now see here," she flared, "who do you think you've got here? You can't order me around like that! If I feel like leaving the key, all well and good. And if I don't, you'll stand for it and like it. You made enough trouble for me the other night as it was."

"We can get away with murder, honey," I assured her dreamily, "we're both young and have our health. Oh, how I wish this phone were out of the way and there was nothing between your lips and mine!"

She sighed good-naturedly and said, "I'll leave the key. But, Wade, please be careful what you do. I don't want to have to go around looking for a job."

"You're as sweet as you are good-looking," I groaned elatedly. "You can count on me. I won't go near the phone, I won't even light the lights if you don't want me to—"

"All right," she said, "then that's that. What you're really doing is spoiling the whole first part of my evening, but I know that doesn't cut any ice with you as long as *yours* is all set."

"Oh," I said, "so that's where I stand! Just knowing that I'm waiting for you up at the place is enough to spoil your evening for you, is it? I sure stand in thick with you and no mistake."

"Now wait," she said, "don't jump down my throat like that. What I meant was simply this: if I let you wait for me up at the place, you'll be on my mind. I'll be afraid something'll go wrong, that you'll give yourself away or give me away; I can't relax with something like that on my mind."

"Suppose you save your relaxing until the end, when we're alone together," I suggested.

"I'll think about it," she said, and laughed. "Let's get this straight now—you want me to leave the key with the downstairs doorman and tell him that a gentleman will call for it. Then you want to go upstairs and wait for me in the place until I get in. Is that it?"

"That's the ticket."

"Okay, then," she said by way of good-bye, "and try not to get ashes all over the rugs, will you? I'll be seeing you."

And then, where her voice had been there was only silence and insulated wire and an invisible gum-chewing individual with earpieces clamped to her head, and I was alone once more. I dropped another nickel in and had Maxine.

"Oh, is that you?" she said at once. "It's ten after six; hurry up, will you? I've got the chops on already. Where you talking from?"

"You mean where'm I listening from, don't you?" I corrected. "I haven't had a chance to say a word so far. Shut up a minute and I'll explain where I am and why I'm not coming home."

"Not *coming!*" she squalled. "Well, this is a fine time to let me know about it! I just got through spending seventy-nine cents at the butcher and the grocer—"

So I didn't go home that Wednesday evening, but I went to a barber shop and got a shave, and the setting sun shining through the plate-glass window struck gleams of emerald, garnet, topaz, and amethyst from the bottles of tonic standing in a row on the counter and made the barber shop seem a jewelry shop to me. And the radio over the door hummed ever so softly about love, the world's one great interest, saying, "Here I am with all my bridges burned, just a babe in arms where you're concerned; oh, lock the doors and call me yours—"

And I kept thinking, "Yes, make the part straight, her eyes are going to look at it. Yes, put talcum on the back of my neck, her fingers may rest there for a minute. Yes, wipe my forehead clean with your towel, it may lean against hers. Sure, hold up the mirror in back of me, so I can see what she sees, and wonder if the love shows through the way it should, like a candle in a paper lantern." All this and more. And to him I suppose I was just another customer, not the man who loved Bernice Pascal!

So I came out of there smelling sweet, looking neat, and striding wide, one hand in my pocket jingling coins, the other at the back of my neck to make sure he hadn't overlooked any little hairs. He hadn't, but what difference did it make? A few days from now they'd all be back there again anyway. But tonight was tonight, and it was sure a sweet night, that was all that mattered. The whole city seemed full of others like me, coming out of barber shops all dolled up to keep their dates with their little loves. Men in gray suits, men in blue suits, men in brown suits, all looking alike, all in love with someone, all heading for where that someone was. And some were whistling, and some were intent on the ground before them, and some glanced into every mirror along the way to catch their own reflections, and some bumped into you and apologized with a friendly smile, others bumped into you and gave you a scowl, still others bumped into you and didn't even know you were there at all— all according to their various temperaments. And out of all the beauty parlors came an endless stream of those little someones whom this was all about, with brand-new permanent waves and glistening water waves, with shimmering manicures and rose-leaf facials, with orange lips and cherry lips and mauve lips, all wearing little skullcaps and little kilts for skirts—some looking at their wristwatches and some at their mirrors and some at the heavens above (as though to judge just how long *he* had been waiting by now). All the players were ready for the game of love, and the endless file of taxicabs bobbing through every street, so repetitious in all their motions, were like a chorus of unlovely but agile Tiller dancing girls to the rest of the proceedings.

Lights flashed out where lights had no business to be—on the blank side walls of buildings and in midair—without giving the day a chance to die decently, so that the twilight was done to death with splashes of tropical yellow, scarlet, and green that moved, that sputtered, flashed and blinked. At the end of one of the side streets a brazen comet flashed by halfway between the roofs and the ground carrying a long tail of lights with it—an elevated train headed uptown. The streets were a kaleidoscope; every drug store, every millinery shop, had its glowing neon tubes of jade and vermilion spelling out what it had to say and dyeing the pavement in front of it, and the throngs that went by on the sidewalk took on for a minute a tinge of greenish or of reddish hue until they had gone on to the next to become some other color, like chameleons. Only directly overhead, if you threw your head back as far as it would go, was anything serene, and there a round blush moon that had been unobtrusively present since four in the afternoon now stood out like a porthole in a chaotic stateroom, with no one able to reach it and look through to the other side. Evening had descended upon New York.

I had a roast beef sandwich and a cup of coffee at a counter shaped like an 8, with waitresses in little yellow linen dresses on the inside and the customers seated on revolving seats around the outside. Which proved nothing at all as far as the sandwich was concerned, but I was in a trance anyway and wouldn't have known whether it was shoe leather or ambrosia I was eating. And when the handmaiden in yellow asked me whether I would like some more coffee, I drew back my cuff and answered that it was a little after seven.

"I'm certainly glad of that," she answered tartly, "and now while I have the perk right here with me, maybe you'll let me know if you can stand another cupful."

So I stood another cupful to kill time, and while its inkiness grew cold before me, kept making mental calculations, although people were standing up in back waiting for seats, mine included. "Now," I said to myself, "she is out somewhere eating with somebody (hope he chokes!) If he's the one she's going out with, then nine chances to one she's dressed already for the evening and won't go back to the place any more. But if she's going out alone or with some one else, then maybe she'll get rid of whoever she's with now and rush back to change. Then if I stick around, I may have a chance to see her before she goes out. It's worth trying." So I paid my check and got out of there, and went up to Fifty-Fifth Street to the tall white building Bernice lived in. But I approached it on the opposite side of the street, and when I had located her floor and the windows that I judged to be hers, they were pitch-dark; no one was in. So I crossed over, and the doorman spun the door around for me, and I found myself in her lobby, with its hidden flesh-colored lighting and its uncomfortable Italian furniture and its chocolate hallman the envy of his race in kid gloves, padded shoulders, and gilt braid. "Yessir," he said, "good evening."

"Phone up Miss Pascal for me, will you?" I said.

"Miss Pascal?" he said. "She stepped out just about fifteen minutes ago."

"Alone?" I said.

He looked at me without smiling and answered, "I couldn't say."

"Oh, yes, you could," I insisted, and slipped something into one of his kid palms, at the same time wishing him all sorts of calamities but without telling him so.

"She left with a gentleman," he said.

The pink lights weren't as pink as they had been until now, "That's all right," I remarked. It wasn't at all. "She left her key with you, didn't she?"

"I didn't know it was that," he said naïvely. "She left a little envelope with me and told me a gentleman would call for it later on. Is that you?"

"That's me, all right," I answered disgustedly. I saw I'd made a mistake by mentioning the key, she hadn't wanted him to know what it was. But in any case, he would have seen me go upstairs in the elevator to her floor and, knowing she was out, surmised the rest. And who the hell was he, anyway?

I tore the little white envelope he passed me open right there under his eyes and shook out Bernice's brass latchkey, which was all it contained. Not a word, or anything. But maybe she hadn't had time. "I'm going up," I said, and he clicked a little metal snapper he held between his fingers, and a lot of Florentine bas-relief done in bronze and copper slid out of the way, and I stepped in the car.

Going up, I thought the ghost of her Narcisse Noir still lingered in the corners of the car; I was sure it was her elusive perfume that I caught with each prolonged breath. I hissed so, trying to draw it to my nostrils, that the starter even turned his head and glanced back over his shoulder at me, evidently under the impression I was either sobbing softly or suffering from a cold in the head. I lowered my eyes.

He stopped the car a trifle above her floor, meticulously lowered it again an inch or two to the right level, opened the slide for me, and I stepped out. I waited until he had hidden himself again and gone down (as a little lighted garnet above the shaft door indicated) before I took out her key and got ready to enter. First I took the precaution of ringing the bell. No one answered it. So then I put the key in the door and let myself in.

I took my hat off before I even crossed the threshold, because here was where she lived, here was where my dreams began. All respect, all homage to love.

And now magic began, and the world dropped away behind me as I carefully, tenderly shut her door after me. The air around me was the air she had breathed all morning, all afternoon; the floor, the rug I moved across was where her feet had carried her a hundred times a day. Oh, everything in here she had touched before me, and so I went around touching chairs and cushions, mirrors, tabletops and doorknobs, light chains and cigaretteboxes, holding a communion with her through the medium of my coarse, yellowed, banal fingers. And when I found her handkerchief in a corner of a divan, I put it to my mouth there in the dark and kissed it lingering. Until the horrible thought presented itself: it may belong to the maid! I nearly retched for a minute, and couldn't wait until I had scratched a match and held it up and searched the corners of it. In one corner it had B. That was all right then, so I whipped out the match and drew the handkerchief to my mouth once more and kissed it again and kissed it again, and put it in my inside pocket. And not being a very intelligent man, all the poetry my mind was capable of at the moment was: "Gee, I love you; I wish you would come home."

I didn't light the electricity because she had asked me not to over the phone that afternoon, as some one who knew her and knew her windows from the street might pass and look up and think she was home and decide to drop in, etcetera. But I didn't really need lights anyway, because in the living room the portières were drawn far back, exposing the whole of each window, and the night was so bright, it made a swath of blue across the floor from each window, like twilight in a grotto when the day is dying outside. I stepped over and looked out without opening the window, and the moonlight lighted my face up and fell across my tie and shirt like one of those diagonal ribbons foreign diplomats are so fond of wearing. There were stars out there too, and city lights, but the moon was the whole cheese. It looked to me from where I was exactly like a gilt thumbtack nailing the blue plush carpet that was the sky closer to the floor of heaven. As I thought of Bernice and wondered where she was, I could almost feel its light swimming in my eyes like soft golden tears. Here was the moon and here was I—why wasn't she here? She would only come home when the moon was gone, perhaps, and something of perfection would be lacking. But even in the dusk of moonrise, how could her arms seem anything but white?

I got so lonely standing there thinking about her that I had to get out of the moonlight. I went back into the depths of the room, with its two funnels of sapphire blue spilled across the floor, and I felt weak all over and my knees begged me not to move any more and my blood felt like honey that is about to run over the edge of a saucer, so sweet, so lazy, so slow. I threw myself face downward on the divan where I had found her handkerchief before, and took the handkerchief out of my pocket and pressed it between my shut eyes and groaned, I think, aloud.

When I had quieted down, I lit a cigarette and stayed there like that for a long, long while, with just a spark of red in front of me that ebbed and glowed again as I drew upon it. And when the heat began to reach my nails and I knew that I better drop it, I found something to drop it in, and then I got up and found the radio and fumbled with it until I had it going and its midget amber bulb shone through the dial into my face. And while it was warming itself up, I felt my way to the telephone and got the downstairs operator on the line. "What time you got down there?" I asked him.

"Twenty to ten," I heard him say. That was what my watch said too, but I had been praying that it would be slow. Gee, there was a long time to go yet.

"I want some sandwiches sent up to Miss Pascal's," I added. Might as well do that now, I thought, and have it over with in case she really *did* come home early. "Is there a delicatessen handy?"

He told me there was a drugstore right in the building. "Good," I said. "Send them up with the elevator boy," and then I told him just what kind I wanted. And I thought, "If she *doesn't* like olives and pimento, I can always send down for some other kind. In that way I'll find out exactly which kind she likes most, and I'll always remember it."

I hung up and decided to mix some drinks for the two of us, and turned off the radio because it was singing a sad love song and this was going to be a night for happy love. I found that the serving pantry didn't have any window, so after shutting its two doors I could light the light in there without any danger. Its flashy brightness blinded me for minutes, and I had to shade my eyes until I got used to it. Then I pulled a couple of trayfuls of ice cubes out of the Frigidaire, found the Gordon Dry where Tenacity (no doubt) kept it—on the floor of the broom closet—and began to peel oranges and lemons with my cuffs rolled back. I was happy and I was whistling with my head bent over my task.

After a while the bell rang, and the fellow with the sandwiches was standing at the door. I took them from him and, happening to lift up a corner of one, found that it was spread with crescents of cucumber. "I ordered olive and pimento," I told him with repugnance.

He had a wearied air, I thought, as of some one who had gone through this trial many times before. "Yessir, half of 'em *are* olive and pimento," he explained. "The others are for Miss Pascal; they're the only kind she eats. They weren't *all* for you, were they?" This last had a matter-of-fact intonation to it, as though no answer were really required.

"Oh, so your counterman has what kind she likes down pat?" I said grimly. "She must send down pretty often."

He smiled out of the corner of his mouth. "Yessir, she does," he said.

"For two, I s'pose."

"Always," he said, and if he had winked I was going to run my hand into which ever eye did it, but he didn't wink, just looked worldly-wise and bored.

I paid him and closed the door, and went back to the serving pantry not so happy as I had left it. For one thing, I had stopped whistling. I was in there quite a while, because I kept tasting the drinks as I mixed them, and consequently I had to keep making them over again. When I had finally accumulated two braces of two each, I quit and carried them inside and set them down next to the sandwiches. Then I put the lights out and sat down there in the dark, with just me and the moon. "Boy, how you're getting wasted!" I remarked to it aloud. After about five or ten minutes, I started to munch one of the sandwiches; that made me thirsty, so I had to sip one of the drinks along with it. By the time I put the empty glass down, the drink had made me hungry, so I had to start munching a second sandwich.

My arm was beginning to ache a little by now from lifting it to my face to look at the time so much, so I unstrapped my wristwatch and laid it down in front of me among the glasses. The whole dial of it vanished at that distance from my eyes, and just the twelve little glowing numbers arranged in a circle remained, with the two little glowing hands aiming at 9 and at 12. Not that

that meant nine, it meant quarter to twelve. "She'll be here before midnight," I told myself. "Maybe she'll come in on the hour, like Cinderella." And I had another drink. But they moved so quick, those hands! The minute hand deliberately skipped 10, 11, and 12, and took a flying leap down to 1 under my very eyes. So she hadn't come in on the hour, after all. And now it was a new day. But it was the same old night.

A vagabond cloud about the size of a fist passed over the moon and immediately turned silver all around the edges as though it had caught fire. "Sure," I encouraged it, "hide the damn thing! What good is it doing me?"

Oh, I was sore at everything right then: the moon, and the night, and myself most of all! "Here I sit," I mumbled, "when if I was a man I'd get up, slam the door, and never come 'round her again. Who does she think she is?" But something inside me whispered, "Maybe you love her because she treats you this way. Maybe she's wise, maybe she knows you better than you know yourself." So I went to the window, and I went to the door. And then I sat down again. And I had another sandwich. And I had another sandwich. And I had another sandwich.

Then, when there was only one left, it occurred to me too late that that wasn't enough to offer her with any propriety. I should have thought of that before when there were two, but now there was only one, and offering her one would be a slight. It would look much better if there weren't any in sight, than to have just the remaining one staring her in the face, seeming to say, "Take me or leave me." So I reached out and picked it up and ate it, slowly, thoughtfully, mournfully—and the little dream of a midnight snack to be shared by the two of us dissolved in crumbs and went the way of all my other dreams, big and small. I know it would have made a swell comedy scene, but I wasn't looking in a mirror, and so my heart sang a blue song while I sat there and chewed.

Then I wiped my mouth on the back of my hand, and I dusted my knees, and I heaved a deep sigh that seemed to come up from my feet. And *still* she didn't come home. I had given up believing that she would ever come home; I was almost beginning to doubt that there was a Bernice.

When I thought of how much I thought of her—why, my head nearly cracked. She was everything to me in one. She was my God, my Garbo. She was dearer to me than a sandwich at Reuben's, sweeter than a soda at Schrafft's. I would rather have looked at her than at the Ziegfeld Follies, rather have folded her in my arms than folded a ten-grand check, rather have held her hand than held a royal flush. It was wicked, it was wild, it was swell.

The hands of the clock were at 8 and at 1 now; I turned it over on its face to try and stop looking at it so much, but that didn't do much good. I kept turning it over all the time, anyway. Finally I put an end to the agony by picking it up by the end of its strap, carrying it to the window, and pitching it out into the night. I don't know where it landed, never heard a sound. After it was gone, I remembered how Maxine had slipped it under my pillowcase the first Christmas Eve after we were married. That made me twice as glad I had done it. And immediately afterward, as though I had dispelled a charm in getting rid of the watch that way, I turned from the window just in time to see the door open and close again noiselessly at the far end of the apartment. Not a sound, just a chink of light there, then gone again.

In the dark she came back to me, in the dark she came home. Into the blue-black emptiness of the room she stepped, with only me there; where there had been nothing before, now there was something, and my temples beat like tom-toms and strange pulses I never knew I had, in strange places like my neck and back of my ears, throbbed delightedly as though they were calling her to my attention—"Oh, Wade, she is here!" As though I didn't know it! As though my mind needed the dumb mechanical parts of me to tell it!

I got so excited, I could hardly see her any more; a sort of rose-red mist swept over her and hid her from my eyes. Then presently she emerged from it again, but her image was still limned in coral like a motionless white statue in a garden flushed by a hidden carmine reflector at its base. Then she spoke, and as her voice flashed into my ears, the peculiar rigidity of a statue that my inflamed senses had given her changed into the mobility of a Bernice coming home to her apartment as she did on any other night, brushing her hair from her eyes with the back of her hand, carrying the same hand to her shoulder to rid it of the short velvet jacket that hung over it, and then with the other hand touching a certain spot on the wall and making the whole place grow light with a sort of jazz dawn, instantaneous and blinding, of lamps and brackets on the walls.

"I thought it was you," she had said, just as the lights went on, "but I never can be sure. I'm a little drunk." The little velvet cape that she had dislodged from one shoulder still clung to the other, hanging like a pennant toward the floor. She twitched, and down it went, sliding off her like a snake and lying coiled around her feet. I stooped to pick it up, and then I stayed there. "Don't," she said. "Don't kiss my knees; Lincoln freed the slaves," and bending over, touched my face with a little gesture that was half a slap and half caress. "Oh, I'm so tired, Wade," she said. "I've had this all night long, in every room I went into to get away from someone in the room before. After all, I couldn't spend the evening in the bathroom sitting on the rim of the tub—" And then she pushed my shoulders back a little and stepped out of the circle of my arms. "I want to be alone a little, and just talk to someone from across a room. Oh, I like love, I even love love, but for just a minute I want to feel nothing but air on all sides of me. So go back there in a chair and drink and look at me if you want to, make your love by remote control."

"What can I say now," I said, "that hasn't been said to you in a corner by someone else this evening? Oh, I get the breaks. I'm the only one of them all that really means this thing; they're all stealing my stuff from me, but they got their innings first— so it must seem to you the other way 'round. Oh, isn't there someone can tell you for me, make you believe me? Oh, if you only had a girlfriend, I could win her over to my side—"

"Get up from the floor," she said; "you have a regular penchant for making passes from your knees."

"Oh, I need help—Bernice, Bernice. The touch of your hand on my face is telegraphed all over me. Can't you see I'm half crazed? You've got to get me out of this state—"

She laughed a little, and then she said, "How am I to blame? It's in you, and in all of them, to torture the life out of some poor girl. And because you came across me, you react like a caged chimpanzee and then try to tell me *I* got you into the state you're in. That's a laugh!"

"Ah, but don't you know it only too well!" I cried, and I reached behind me for my glass, which still had something in it, and pitched the liquor into her face. I saw the whole thing so clearly, like in a slow-motion film, even saw the gin hiss through the air in sort of a funnel shape and break over her face and shoulders in little drops. And even while it was happening, I didn't know why I had done it, wished I hadn't done it. I suppose I wanted to kiss her so badly and have her near me, and she wouldn't let me at the moment, so the effort to make her a part of me took that form on account of the increased distance between us, and I threw the liquor at her instead of throwing my arms around her.

She started up, but before her knees could quite carry her all the way to a standing position, I was over there and my arms were around her. I squeezed her, and I buried the words she was saying with my lips. She tried to struggle a little at first, and then because (as she herself had said) she loved love, she stopped and stood quietly with her mouth to mine. And all the way from where her fragile spike heels touched the floor up to where her lips shared their rouge with mine, she was a lightning rod of love; she was what she had been born for: something that caused a short circuit.

And later she said, "Oh, this thing tortures us, doesn't it? All our lives through we're never rid of it. And nothing that we say or do can be held against us, can it, because we're not responsible, are we?"

In the dawn, the world started over again, carrying New York with it as it rushed eastward to meet the sun. Her eyes, then, catching the light from the brightening skies outside before anything else in the room, were like two white pebbles gleaming upward through fathoms of murky water. She shut them a minute and breathed deeply. She said, "Wade." I took her hands and clasped them around me, behind my back. She said, "I love you. I knew I would. I told you I would. I do."

I had loved her so long, so much, it really didn't matter by now whether she loved me or not. It was just the third button to a two-button suit.

"Oh, I don't know for how long," she said. "Not forever. Maybe only just for now. But while it's here, while I've got it—!" She kissed me two or three times on the face. "I want to give you the first token of it, the one true token, the only token. Listen."

I listened.

"Will you do something for me? For your own sake?"

I asked her what it was.

"Do it for me, Wade. Try to do it." She seemed so afraid to come to the point. She brushed the back of her hand all around her face, almost exactly the way cats do when they wash. "I don't know how to say it."

"Say it; what are you afraid of? What is it?"

"Because you won't believe me; you won't take it in good faith."

I shrugged. "All I can do is try."

"You see, I love you—"

"Lucky me." She put her hand over my mouth. "Let me finish, or I won't be able to go on at all. I said I loved you, didn't I? Well, that changes everything. While I was still in the act of falling for you, I didn't think about you much, just myself. Now I'm thinking about you more than myself. Wade, will you do me a favor? Don't see me any more."

"So you feel like kidding, do you?"

She moaned disconsolately. "Oh, I knew it. I knew it. You don't understand. It's because I *love* you!"

"Well, in that case, how about taking a dislike to me, so I can stick around?"

She nodded and put her hand on my arm in quick, nervous agreement. "Exactly. If I disliked you, the dirtiest trick I could play you would be to have you around me all the time. Wanna know why?"

"May as well," I said, "the show at the Palace is rotten this week."

"Oh, if I could only illustrate it concretely," she said, "but I can't! It's just a feeling, a surmise. I know you won't believe it. But I have a hunch, oh, such a hunch, honey, that if you get in too thick with me you're coming to a quick, bad finish. You're different from the types I've gone around with. Oh, you do the things that all men do, but Wade, you're *clean*, you're *straight*. Those are always the ones that get it in the neck!"

"I don't follow you," I said grouchily. "What do you do, associate with crooks?"

"*I* don't, *personally*," she said meekly. And then, all anxiety again. "Wade, won't you break away? *I'll* go on loving you. Maybe forever that way and not just for today."

"You could tell me that you don't want me, that would be squarer. Look," I said, wheeling around toward her, "you tell me honestly that you don't want me, and I'll go, I'll do what you want. Is that a go?" And I slipped the knot of my tie determinedly up to the base of my throat, where it belonged.

"I can't tell you that," she said dismally, "it wouldn't be true." Then suddenly she flared up furiously at no one in particular and flung one of her embroidered mules violently across the room by the heel. "What is this love racket? I'd rather have a baked apple! Get this and keep it got," she said, turning to me. "As I understand love, I love you. I don't want to have anything to do with your laundry, don't want you around me every day, but how I love you is nobody's business!

"So stay if you must, honey," she said after a while, "but tomorrow I won't love you any more."

I only laughed. "I'll take my chances. Who could be a big enough fool to let *you* slip out of his life?"

"Poor Wade," she said pensively, "good-bye to *you!*"

CHAPTER THREE

Tomorrow she didn't love me any more. And tomorrow, and tomorrow. But that was all right; at least I was with her, if only to hear her say so.

"She *is* in, I tell you!" I barked at Tenacity. "I just heard her say to you, 'Go see who's at the door.'"

This startling revelation so robbed Tenacity of her presence of mind that by the time she had recovered it, I, at any rate, was in, whether Bernice was or not. "You're certainly *stubborn*," she commented disgustedly, shaking her head after me. "If it was me, I wouldn't *want* to come in after they told me—"

"But I haven't got your finesse," I interrupted, crossing my legs in the chair.

"I'll say you haven't—nor anybody else's!" Bernice agreed tempestuously from the doorway of her room.

I turned to Tenacity. "You see, she *was* in after all."

Tenacity scratched her head as though intensely surprised at this fact herself.

"Maybe I am in," Bernice continued, "but I'm going out so fast that about all you'll get is the breeze as I pass you by." Whereupon she commenced putting this threat into operation by entering at one door and crossing the room diagonally toward the other, the outside one. Without looking at me. She was dressed informally for the evening, in something that had big peach-colored flowers printed all over it, and she had a little cap on made up of shiny black discs all sewn together. And she looked good to the eye—but wasn't kind to the ear. "Never mind, stay right where you are," she said with false solicitude. "I'll be seeing you some other time."

But I got in front of her just the same. "No, you'll be seeing me now," I said.

"I knew it would come to that," she said. "Give them an inch and they take a yard." And she gave Tenacity a hard, calloused laugh.

I gave Tenacity a hard, dirty look and she ambled out of the room with the cryptic remark, "I'd rather be a nun *any*time."

"What's the matter," I said, "ain't I even good enough to talk to any more?" And I put my hands on her arms and turned her persuasively around the other way, away from the door. She just laughed a little more, and found a chair and sat in it, with her legs crossed up to her waist.

"Oh, it isn't that," she said, and waved her head wearily.

"What is it, then?"

"You walk in like this, unannounced, and expect me to drop everything—"

"I phoned you first, and you weren't in."

"I *was* in," she snapped. "I've been in since lunch."

"Well, you didn't come to the phone yourself, and the room was full of voices—"

She clenched her little fists over the arms of the chair. "They're coming back, too. That's why I wanted to get out. While I had the chance. I'm sick of them." And then she said, like a sad little girl who's been promised something three Christmases away, "I've been invited to a party, and I thought I'd go."

"Who are *they?*" I asked. "What do you use this place for, some sort of a hangout?"

She made an upward gesture with her hand, from her chest to her chin, as though she were fed up about something. "Don't ask me to explain," she said indifferently.

She seemed so tired all of a sudden, so inert, sitting there like that, all dressed for going out and yet not minding terribly much whether she went or whether she didn't. Her head was back a little ways, and her eyes were looking up at the invisible line where the ceiling met the opposite wall. She was thinking about something. Her foreshortened upper lip came down over her lower one and hid it, rouge and all, so that her mouth almost disappeared for awhile, leaving just a short pink scratch. I had never seen her like that before; so tired and all. I felt sorry for her. I went over to her and lifted one of her hands to my mouth and began to munch it. Only the slight rising and falling of the big peach flowers across her chest told that she was alive at all.

She took her hand away and let it pass gently down the side of my arm. "You're nice, Wade," she said. "I'm never scared with you."

I couldn't understand what she meant by that, but then, still without moving, she said, "I'll have to go. You can't stay here either."

"Why?"

"Because you can't. Because I don't want you to. Because—because I *still* care more for you than others I know."

"What's the good talking, Bernice," I said gently, "unless you say things I can understand?"

She turned and looked at me with a mocking little smile. "Do you want to go for a ride?" she said.

Thinking she was proposing it, I said, "What do you say we do?" with cheerful alacrity.

She shuddered comically. "God forbid! Just stay here on the premises about an hour longer—"

I had started to say "Will you come back?" when the speaking tube out in the foyer buzzed with alarming vehemence, as though it were about to split in two.

With that, all tiredness left her, fright took its place, and she started up from where she was sitting, caught me by the hand somehow, and had me at the door with her before I could grasp what it was all about. She opened it and listened, although there was no one there. I looked over her shoulder. A little jewel-like white light over the elevator door flashed on and twinkled impudently at us.

"That was from downstairs," she said. "Come on. If I don't go now, I won't get out all evening." And she edged me aside and closed the door behind us.

"Wait a minute," I said surlily, "are you giving me the bum's rush, or what?" But looking at her face, I wondered if it really was paler than it had been a little while ago, or did I just imagine it?

"Don't fight with me *now,* Wade," she pleaded huskily. "Come downstairs with me; it'll be all right."

"Yeah, but you're going to a party; why couldn't I have waited in the place for you until you got back?" I insisted.

"You come with me," she said then. "Anything, *anything*—only don't *stand* here!" Suddenly the little white light had gone out.

I suppose that, all unwittingly, I had just practiced a form of blackmail on her; I don't imagine she had intended me to go to the party with her at all. She crossed the corridor a little to the left of the elevator shaft and flung open the door to the emergency staircase.

"Aren't you going to wait for the elevator?" I asked.

"Get it from the floor below," she answered, and started down the cement steps. The staircase door began to drift back after her on its heavy hinges. "Don't stand there, Wade, don't stand there!" she called back hollowly. I went after her and down the first five or six steps and then, at shoulder-level to the floor, stopped to glance back over my shoulder. The elevator door, to the right and now hidden from me, shot open and slapped a big gob of honey-colored light across the checkered tiled flooring to the base of the wall, and all the way up it. And set right in the middle of this light, like a design in a stained-glass window, was a shadow that looked like a hydra or centipede or octopus, with many legs, one thick body, and then on top of that, numerous heads. Or in other words, a group of people standing so closely together in the car as to be indistinguishable. Before they could move or separate, the lazy staircase door finally reached the end of its arc and fitted noiselessly back into place, wiping the corridor out. I turned again and went on down and joined Bernice on the floor below. She had been holding the door down there open for me, but more out of anxiety than politeness, I could tell.

"I told you not to stand there," she said. "People don't use the emergency staircase—they'd know right away—"

And giving the door into my keeping, she went over and pushed the button, summoning the elevator. It came at once, having only to descend from the floor above, and when we stepped in there were still layers of haze in it and an odor of rancid cigars. I looked down at the floor, but all there was there was a celluloid toothpick some one had dropped.

"I moved down to the floor below," Bernice explained derisively to the car operator. "Sure; cut a hole in the floor and dropped through with my chum here. And I went out hours ago, get *that* straight." And then, turning to me, she said quite audibly, "Give him something."

I felt like saying, "Why should Harlem fatten on the peccadilloes of Fifty-Fifth Street?" But I gave him a one-dollar bill folded over many times to look like a whole lot more. By the time he got through disentangling it, we would be far away.

"It's on Fifty-Fourth," she said to me as we left the door.

"Let's walk it," I suggested affably.

She looked at me thunderstruck. "You're with Bernice, Wade," she reminded me.

So we got in a taxi and it started west, that being the kind of a street Fifty-Fifth was. And came to Sixth Avenue and couldn't turn left on account of an opening (or maybe it was a closing) at the Ziegfeld Theater. Then when we came to Seventh, the driver ignored it for reasons best known to himself, and proceeded blithely on to Broadway. "What was the matter with Seventh?" I inquired through the glass shutter.

"If you coulda made a turn there, you're a wizard," he informed me.

"Why, I coulda swung a Mack truck and three coal barges around in the room you had," I said.

"Oh, let him alone," Bernice said irritably. "What difference does one block more make?"

I could've answered that easily, knowing just what amount I had in my pocket, but preferred not to.

When we came to Broadway, no left turns were allowed. We stood there helplessly, while the whole of New York north of Fifty-Ninth Street filed by in conveyances of one sort or another. When the migration had been thoroughly completed, and not until then, we were allowed through. By the time we reached Eighth Avenue, I was fully prepared to lean out and swerve the wheel left with my own hands, even if it caused a collision, but the driver finally turned it himself. He then turned his head, bestowed a glance of approbation on Bernice's legs, and inquired of them, "What number did you say, lady?"

"Here I am, up here, not down there," she instructed him, and gave him the address a second time.

"That's over by Third," he commented philosophically.

So that to reach Third Avenue from Sixth, we had to go as far as Eighth and then double back. It's incredible, but then it's New York.

My money had dropped behind the meter before we had even got as far as Sixth a second time. When we finally got out in front of the place we were going to, I was a dollar and a half short. So I told him to wait, and I went in to find the doorman, because it was one of those new buildings that have their doormen engaged before the steel beams are even up. But none was in sight. Meanwhile Bernice was powdering her face in front of a glass hanging on the wall. So I went out again to the driver and explained matters to him. I did this merely as a matter of form, expecting momentarily to have to repeat the story to a policeman. To my, not only surprise but almost consternation, he didn't even suggest such a thing. "I know the lady you got with you pretty well by sight," he explained, "I often pick her up in front of her house." There was a camaraderie about this that I didn't exactly like, but my hands were tied, so to speak. "I mean, as a fare," he assured me. "My stand's on her corner." I had to ignore the unintentional impudence of his attempting to reassure me as to Bernice's loyalty, or whatever you want to call it. I gave him my name and address, and corroborated it by producing a number of envelopes and papers from my inside pocket. He wrote it down and said he would stop by for the balance of the fare the next time he was "out that way."

"No, no," I interposed, "this is just to show you who I am; so you'll know I'm on the level. I'll give it to you at your stand, on the corner."

"Yeah, but suppose I'm not there?" he objected.

But I was sick of him by now, so I said, "I'll find you, don't worry," and went in to Bernice. She was doing a tap dance on one leg, holding her dress up to her thighs.

We went up in an automatic elevator to the roof, passed under the open sky for an instant, and then were indoors again in a one-story stucco bungalow. No one came forward to greet us. Bernice suddenly left my side, opened a door revealing a bedroom with white furniture and pink hangings, and went in with the remark, "You go in *there.*" I couldn't make out where *there* might be, so I stayed where I was and waited for her.

Shortly afterward, a beautiful, unprepossessing, black-haired person passed beyond an open doorway at the back of the dwelling and glanced casually out. My presence didn't register in time to halt her progress at the moment, but a second later she was back again for another look, had turned, and was coming toward me. She bore a length of white stuff sewn with glass along with her, but it didn't hide anything of much importance. "Didn't Jerry give you your money yet?" she remarked irritably.

I turned around and looked behind me to see who she was talking to, but there was no one there. By the time I turned again, she was standing before me. "How much is it?" she said then, "I have to do everything myself around here!"

I must have looked blank, because she sighed as one with the patience of a kindergarten teacher and said slowly and distinctly, "How—much—is—the stuff? Or don't you talk English?"

"I'm not the bootlegger," I grinned.

"Well, then, who are you?" she said.

"I came with Bernice," I said.

"Well, who's Bernice?" she wanted to know.

My nerves snapped and I said, "What's the matter, don't you live here?"

"Do I live here?" she echoed. "Are you telling *me?*" And then turning her head toward where she had just come from, she emitted an appalling quantity of noise, a combined scream and bellow, as though I had attempted to assault her. *"Jerry!"* I nearly jumped out of my socks.

But instead of a man rushing excitedly out there to protect her, a tawny-haired girl came hurriedly into view and said, "Did you want something, Marion?"

"Yes, I do," Marion declared positively. "Do you know any one named Bernice?"

"Which Bernice?" inquired Jerry. "I know a Bernice Fairchild and I also know—"

"Oh, for Jesus' sake, Bernice," I roared toward the door, "will you please come out here and tell these dumb broads something!"

Instantly I saw a gleam of admiration light each of their four eyes; evidently calling them broads was the "open sesame." I was the sort of person they were used to having around. Their hauteur dissolved before my eyes; they seemed to relax. Bernice opened the door and came out, her features barely peering forth through snowdrifts of powder. "Oh, hello, Bernice," Jerry said, "I didn't know you were here!" Bernice took her aside and said something to her; I had a distinct impression she was explaining my presence in terms of "I didn't know what to do with him so I brought him along." Jerry tactlessly allowed her eyes to stray toward me, and I heard her say: "Leave it to me."

Jerry announced to the other girl, "She knew Sonny Boy," meaning Bernice. This was evidently by way of introduction, for I saw them shake hands.

"I only met him once," said Bernice guardedly. "Jerry told me about him and you."

"Twice, pal, twice," Jerry reminded her sweetly. "Once in my place and once—"

"Oh, I don't mind," the one called Marion said. "He's gone now. He's in Detroit."

"She's been sharing expenses with me this last month," Jerry said.

Bernice suddenly without the least provocation whirled around to me and said with a gust of undisguised anger, "For Pete's sake, do you have to be told where the liquor is! Can't you find it?"

So I took it for granted she wanted to be left alone with them, and I strolled off with my hands in my pockets and my head bent unhappily.

In the rear room, ignoring the presence of a number of people who were lolling around in the background, I helped myself to a drink from a bottle that stood on a table. Not alone on the table by any means, but I chose it for its label. After a while I tired of going back to it so much, so I brought it along with me to the radiator box I was sitting on and kept it there until it was no good any more. Then I opened the window behind me and threw it out. About ten minutes later every one in the room got up and ran out toward the door, so I grew curious and went after them. The fat doorman was standing there looking unhappy, with a tall policeman beside him. I heard the latter say that an old lady had just been taken to the hospital with a scalp wound from broken glass. That didn't interest me much; I went back to where I had been sitting and wondered who could have done it. It was only a good while later, after the policeman had been made a present of two bottles of rye and had gone away, that I remembered I had done it. So I stood up excitedly and ran over to Jerry, whom I presumed was one of the hostesses, if you could call them that.

"Listen, do you know who threw that—" I started to say.

She smiled indulgently and said, "Why, you did, of course; everybody saw you do it."

I left her then, but later we were back together again, and she kept getting her head under my chin somehow. "You're always looking around the room for Bernice," I heard her say. "Don't always look around the room for her; she's all right."

Finally I gave her head a strong push, and she fell over on the carpet on her elbows. She stayed there rubbing them, and looked up at me and said, "You're not so dead, after all."

"Quit jazzing around me so much," I told her. "I'm not hot for you."

She laughed and said, "How do you know I'm not for you, though?"

Then all at once the glass I held in my hand gifted me with momentary intuition, and I saw through the whole maneuver. I remembered how Bernice had taken her aside for a minute when we first came in, and said something to her in an undertone; and how she, this one, had looked over in my direction and answered, "Leave it to me." So I realized then that Bernice must have asked her to do her a favor and take me off her hands, vamp me or something, anything that would keep me busy and give her a free rein for the evening. And I thought to myself, "Oh, *yeah?*" But I felt blue and unwanted just the same. And I got up and went out of the place, out into the open air. I went to the back of the roof and sat on the edge of a fire escape with my legs dangling over above a pit a million miles below me. I finished what was in my glass and then I set it down in back of me and lost myself among the lights below, which kept spinning up toward me all the time but never quite reached me. It seemed to me all I had to do was to lean down toward them a little way—and then they would be able to reach me. But I knew better than to do that; so I stopped looking at them, and they all went back to their places far below me. Then I heard a voice say, "Boyfriend, don't sit there; you scare me." I turned around and saw a pair of green-silk-stockinged legs standing there slim and straight. And above them was Jerry again, looking down at me.

I got to my feet and said, "What do you want? What are you following me around for?"

"Can't I like you if I want to?" she said.

I told her that I saw through her, that she was just doing it to do Bernice a favor and keep me away from her.

"That's how it started," she admitted. "She *did* ask me that. But I'm not pretending now; I really like you." And a whole lot more, including suggestions as to my future sleeping quarters.

I spat over the edge of the roof and said, "I didn't even hear that. Where's Bernice, what's she doing now?"

She flamed up like a skyrocket, and I quickly shifted around to the other side of her, thinking she might try to push me over the edge. "Oh, so you want to know, do you, sweet man? Well, she's put herself under the hammer in there for a hundred dollars. Just one big happy family!"

I left her standing there and went in, and that lump in my neck wasn't an Adam's apple, it was my heart. Bernice was standing up on a chair, just winding up some sort of a harangue she'd been giving. And she was very drunk; her hair kept getting in her eyes. "—All privileges included except leaving marks on the lily-white torso," I heard her say. "But it's gotta be in cash, no checks accepted!"

The noise in there was terrific. And at that, not every one was noticing her. But enough were—too many were. I tried to get to her and get her off the chair. Pick it up by one leg and *dump* her off if necessary. But, like in a bad dream, I couldn't get to her; they were all in my way, and the harder I'd push this one and that one, the harder they'd push me back. "Don't fight!" I heard Bernice call out delightedly.

"Bernice!" I shouted over a number of heads, "Do you love me? Don't do that!"

Suddenly all the printed peach-colored flowers left her, collapsed into a circle of rag around her feet. And she'd done it herself. "Oh, it's warm in here, so warm in here!" she shouted.

"Bernice!" I wailed agonizedly, "don't do that! Don't you love me?"

She heard me then, and looked at me, and said, "Have you got a hundred dollars? If you have, then it's all right with me."

"I'll get it, Bernice!" I almost screamed. "I'll get it! Only don't do that!"

I saw her wink at somebody, and she called back, "I'll be waiting for you!"

Outside in the hallway I came up against Jerry, who was just coming in again. "Make her put her dress on," I said, ridding my lapel of her hands. "I'm going to get a hundred dollars, so I can get her away from here."

"You're not a real man," she said scathingly, "or you'd know how to get her away from here without a hundred dollars. And you're not a sweet man, or you'd let her collect and then make her split it with you. I'm wise to you, you're just some sap in love with her. *Real* love!" she grimaced, and flung her hands out after me derisively. "She can *have* you; I'm glad you passed me by!"

The elevator came up to the roof at the rate of a floor a year, but finally it got there, which was something. It went down again like dishwater in a choked-up sink. I tore out of it, and the plump doorman sat up alarmedly on his improvised couch and threw off the plush covering that was a table runner in the daytime. "*Now* what happened up there?" he said, "a murder?"

There were only two things I wanted to know, and I asked him both of them without bothering to answer.

"Twenty to eleven," he said, "and there's a phone right here in the lobby, but the management don't like people to use it for outside calls."

I looked at it, but it was right in the open, had no door, and I didn't want him to listen, so I went out and found a drugstore on the corner. Something told me to get a lot of nickels at the cashier's desk before I went in the booth; something told me I was going to need them. One call, I knew, would never do the trick; I'd have to keep on and on. I carried a fistful in with me and laid them on the little wooden slab under the phone.

The voices and the laughing were still ringing in my ears. Jerry's liquor was still in my stomach, the sweat of agony I had shed those last few minutes, with Bernice up on the chair, still dampened the back of my shirt. And here—not a sound, just me alone, by myself, wondering whom to ring up first.

I took the receiver off and I put the first nickel in, and even as the nickel dropped and rang the bell, I had a sinking feeling to go with it; I knew it wasn't going to be any use. Lending money to friends went out of style with buttoned shoes and mustache cups. But there was nothing like trying. And while I waited, I rapped the back of my hand against the wall of the booth, which was pine. They call that knocking on wood for luck.

Jackie Conway, "the boy who made good," came to the phone. He had stopped being Jackie Conway quite some time before this, and was John Crandall Conway these days. There was only one stage he still had to pass through—the J. Crandall Conway stage. He had even stopped having his phone listed the last few months, but at least he still answered it himself, provided you knew the number. Forgotten was the time I had pretended to look for a room in his rooming house to enable him to smuggle his valise out while the landlady's back was turned.

He was in the midst of a bridge game, he told me, but that was all right, it could wait five minutes. One strange thing about him, he actually *did,* I believe, like to be interrupted by phone calls while he was playing bridge. He thought it gave people the impression that he was much sought-after, a very busy man. And impressions counted for so much in his life.

I told him I had to have a hundred dollars, and could he lend it to me? "Gladly," he said, "I'll expect you to give me an IOU for it, that's all." It all seemed too good to be true.

"You drop around sometime tomorrow—" he went on. "No, tomorrow's Sunday, isn't it. Can you make it Monday morning—?"

I was forced to tell him I couldn't, that I had to have it right tonight, right within an hour, or it wouldn't be any good to me.

"You seem to be in a hurry," he observed. "What's the rush, what's it all about?"

I couldn't tell him that; I know that if I could've, I would have gotten the money from him right then and there. It would have been worth that much to him to be able to repeat so piquant a tale to all his friends, as host and as guest, for many months to come. He loves to play the scandal-monger.

"You in trouble of some kind, Wade?" he went on.

"No, I'm not in trouble, Jackie," I said, "it's just that I've got to have the money."

So then he answered, a little coolly, "I'm afraid I can't do it right tonight, Wade, on such short notice. If you can wait until Monday morning, I'd be only too glad to let you have it. Or if you can give me some inkling as to why you have to have it in such a hurry, I could even borrow it on my own responsibility from one of the boys that are up here with me right now (although I don't like to do that), but I'd really have to know what you want it for before I could do that. It's only fair, don't you think?"

I lost patience then, and growled, "Oh, say yes or no, will you, Jackie, and get it over with! Either you will or you won't. Which is it?"

He said stiffly, "You sound as though I were asking you the favor, instead of you're asking me—"

"I'm asking you the favor, and you're turning me down," I interrupted, "is that right?"

"Unless," he said, "you—"

"Good night," I said formally, and hung up.

Next I tried Billy Cumberland, who came in from Duluth over the weekend seven years ago. He never went back to Duluth again. "Billy," I said, "how's chances of raising fifty dollars?"

So I put another nickel in and called up Eddie Ryan. He'd had a song out three months before, and they were still playing it on the merry-go-rounds at Luna Park. So I congratulated him about it, and he seemed surprised and said, "Wait a minute, are you *sure* I wrote that?" And then it all came back to him and he said, "Oh, sure! I remember now." Upon which I said, "I want to borrow twenty-five dollars from, you, Eddie." "Bring up your decimal point two places," he answered tragically, "and I can accommodate you."

I moved next door into a cooler booth and phoned Phil Broderick, who, being married, is afraid to refuse his friends when they endeavor to borrow money because of what his wife might think and say about him. She used to be a chorus girl. But just that evening, she was either out or out of earshot. He turned me down beautifully, as though he'd been rehearsing what he'd like to say on such an occasion for months past and never had the opportunity to use it before now. Incidentally, I had raised the ante to a full hundred once more, figuring that as long as I wasn't very likely to get it anyway, I may as well try for the whole amount. People have more respect for someone who tries to borrow a hundred dollars than they have for someone who tries to borrow ten. Moreover, it's very often less of a risk; they're likely to get the hundred back, but they're lucky if they ever see the ten again.

I believe I phoned ten people altogether in the space of about twelve or fifteen minutes. I even lost the little tact I had had left and rang one or two who knew me so little I had to explain to them just who I was before I sprang the question. So you can see what chance I had. When there was just one nickel left, I gave it up as a bad job, left the booth, and bought a phosphate at the soda fountain. My throat was dry from talking so much.

The phosphate brought the jag on again a little. I went out and started to walk west without exactly knowing where I was going. I crossed Park, and then Madison and Fifth, just missing being run over by a Town Nash on the last thoroughfare. After which the jag left me for good, and I just felt drawn around the eyes. But the incident gave me an idea, which I pondered for fully half a block before finally rejecting it. It was to get myself hit by some timid, affluent old gentleman's car and settle for a hundred on the spot instead of bringing suit later. The main difficulty was: not to get hit by some one who, after I was all knocked in a heap and no good for the rest of the evening, might prove to be anything but timid or affluent and say, "Go ahead, sue me!" And not to be damaged too badly to be able to get right back to Bernice with the booty. And not to be arrested as a would-be suicide. Outside of which the project was a perfectly good one. So I gave it up.

I turned south on Sixth Avenue and stared up at a passing elevated train for inspiration, but all it gave was a shower of sparks and someone's saliva.

I went to Connie's on Sixth Avenue. After he had let me in, Connie went back behind the bar and said, "Hello, Wade. What can I do for you?" So I looked at the ceiling, I looked at the floor, I looked at the wall in back of me, and I looked at the wall in back of Connie. I spoke, and when I spoke, I put it in the worst possible way, like you always do when you want a thing badly. I said, "I didn't came in here to buy anything. I'm a punk, Connie. I want to borrow a hundred dollars." Connie smiled and said, "You're no punk, 'cause you're not going to get it." So I smiled back and said, "I'm no punk; *you* are," and I went out again on Sixth Avenue.

It had started to rain while I was in there, and the shimmer of the lights looked like yellow torches blazing up out of the wet pavement. But that didn't mean a thing to me; if it had been raining dimes and nickels that would have been a whole lot better. I turned my collar up and shoved my hands into my pockets and thought. I thought of some one I knew: Rapper, the stage manager of the show that had been running the past few months at the Cort. That was near there, too.

Before I was through thinking about him, I was there. My feet must have done it by themselves. I guess they loved Bernice too. I asked for him at the stage door, and the doorkeeper told me I had just missed him, he'd gone home only a minute ago. I thought of chasing after him, but the doorkeeper told me he'd broken his heart and taken a taxi because it was a wet night. Then I asked him where Rapper lived, but he said they weren't allowed to tell things like that. So I said, "What's he afraid of, the Board of Health?" and went out on the sidewalk again.

While I was standing there, the last stragglers of the company came out and went home. A girl by herself, still fixing her garter as she came out of the doorway, and then two girls and a natty fellow who looked as though he'd had his clothes poured over him hot and then allowed to harden.

I thought he was going to get into the taxi with them at first, but after he already had one foot on the running board, he glanced around and seemed to change his mind. He shut the door and they drove off, and he remained standing where he was and staring idly down the street. Then all at once, without even turning to look at me, he said, "Did you want to see Rapper?"

"Why?" I answered hostilely.

"I work with him," he said, "maybe I could do something for you."

"You nor nobody else," I told him, "unless you have a hundred bucks you can fork over for the time being."

He looked up at the sky, which was dry now and full of little silvery clouds, and said: "The gin at the drugstore goes right to one's head."

"I'll be seeing you," I remarked coldly.

So he said, "It may be the effect of the full moon, but you appeal to me to the extent of five dollars. Come along with me and get it."

I felt like saying, "Go on away from me," and help him do so with the end of my foot, and then I thought, "Somebody else has the hundred for her in his pocket right now; oh, don't waste time!" So I took him by the lapel, which seemed to please him, and I said, "Let's go, will you! I don't want a drink, and I don't want any incense burning in Woolworth Buddhas—I only want to go."

We went in a taxi, and every minute my heart said sixty prayers. "Keep her there for me until I get back. I don't know Who or What—but Somebody, Something, keep her there for me until I get back!" We went up a flight of steps, and every step my heart ticked off a prayer.

When he had lit the lights and locked the door, I hit him in the face. He went back into an easy chair that happened to be behind him, and stayed there, with his legs almost at right angles and two ribbons of blood, one from each nostril, dripping down his chin. I went all over the place, and then I came back to where he was. He'd gotten over his dizziness, and he drew his legs in to get up and said, "I'm going to get a policeman."

"Try it," I advised him, "and you'll be telling your story at the stage door of hell."

I went all over the place a second time. I was nervous, and the second time was as much of a waste of time as the first. By the time I got back, he *had* managed to get out of the chair and was fumbling at the door, trying to get it open without attracting my attention. I said, "Get away from there! I don't want to hit you any more; you're all squashy as it is." He dodged aside and quavered, "I didn't do anything to you."

"Where is it?" I said. He asked me what I meant, and when I told him, got kind of wise and answered, "In the National City Bank on Seventy-Second Street, and the doors don't open till nine on Monday."

"You better pray you got some stuck around here some place," I told him, " 'cause if you won't tell me where, I'll hit you, and if you tell me the wrong place to look, I'll hit you, and if you tell me there isn't any, I'll hit you anyway just for luck."

He went a little whiter (or whatever color comes after white, 'cause he was white already) and faltered, "I don't know how much you want."

"All," I said.

He struggled with himself, and I drew my elbow back, and he said, "I have a little in the bathroom, in the crevice behind the tissue paper."

I went right in there, and instead of using his head and getting out the front door while he had the chance, he came right at my heels, whining, "I was saving it for the rent. The show closes Saturday. What am I gonna do?" I was too busy to answer him at the moment. In the little built-in niche, between two tiles, where the putty or whatever it is they use had fallen out, there was a wad of fives and tens. While I was counting them over, he suddenly and belatedly made up his mind to quit the scene and get help. I got him by the shoulder with one hand just in time, and said, "You wait'll I'm out of here before you do your act, get me?" But the interruption had made me lose count and I had to start over again at the beginning. It came to one hundred and fifteen altogether. I was going to leave the last three fives with him, but I reasoned that to get back to the party as quickly as possible I'd have to take a taxi, so I shoved the whole amount in my pocket. He gave a little moan of futile protest and lifted the handkerchief he'd been stopping his nose with to the side of his head. At the same time I caught sight of a lot of sooty water lying in the tub with bits of pink and white underwear floating around in it, and toyed momentarily with the notion of giving him a push into it. But there was no reason to do so, so instead I buttoned my coat, went through the large room, got the door open, and took a quick run down the steps, ending in a vault over the last five or six. He called down after me, "You dirty crook, you'll get yours for this someday!" and then quickly slammed the door of his apartment shut, as though expecting me to turn around and come running back at him. He could have called me much worse than that, for all I'd have cared; he'd just been a means to an end, and I didn't have any more time for him by now. And anyway you look at it, the epithet certainly fitted me. Dirty or otherwise, I had become a crook now for her sake. And did I regret it? I was the happiest crook that ever ran away from the scene of the burglary as I came out into the open and threw my arm at a taxi. Of course, it had some one in it, and the driver snubbed me majestically. I got a free one a moment later, and rearing down the street on what felt to be no more than two wheels, took a look back through the rear pane; there was no one in sight, no sign of commotion, not a whistle had sounded. It was almost no fun.

The driver was one of those nervous New York types who believe in round corners and can only see green, never red. That was all right. No matter haw fast he went, he couldn't go fast enough for me. I had a feeling then that if we had gone into something and I had been smashed up, my heart would have leaped out of my breast and gone on to her alone, with the hundred dollars wrapped around it. But we got there with me still all around my heart, and the hundred in my pocket. The driver took half of the extra fifteen, and I realized that I had no right to argue with him, because after all, I was paying with another man's money.

"I could've got ten tickets on your account," he explained. I contented myself with remarking, "I only wanted to hire your cab, not buy it," and ran in the doorway. He seemed to think I was running indoors because I was afraid of him, and called after me, "Come back and say that to my face." I answered by making a noise with my mouth that really belonged someplace else. Thus we parted dissatisfied with one another.

The young, rotund doorman was busy on the floor with a pail and mop. He looked up with an impersonal scowl and complained, "You tell those ladies up there, if any more of 'em are gonna get sick, to get it over with up on the roof or else wait'll they get out on the street, and not make any more midway stops. This is the third time tonight I've been over this territory!"

"Is the one I brought with me, the one that did the dance down here, still there?" I asked him eagerly.

"Don't ask *me* to keep tabs on 'em," he said aggrievedly. "They'll be coming down in parachutes yet! The only tenants in the building that haven't complained about the noise is the couple that went to Greenwich over the weekend. The station house on Fifty-Third is so tired of getting calls from here that they won't even answer any more." Which argued either that the party had gotten beyond all control since my leaving it or else that he was subject to flights of vivid imagery.

I got the elevator, which unfortunately he had not been able to attend to yet. A vanity compact had been stepped on and burst open in the corner, spraying flowery pink powder over everything. There was also an empty bottle rocking about the floor like on the deck of a boat at sea. And one of the mirrors and the plush seat at the back of the car had something much worse the matter with them. All of which did not make for a pleasant upward journey.

I crossed the roof and entered the bungalow expecting to see some Babylonian orgy in progress, according to the doorman's account. But either he had been carried away by righteous indignation or the chief offenders were those who had left, because there was far less noise than when I had left three-quarters of an hour (or was it a couple of years?) before. Two or three nondescript males of the parasitical variety were still present as long as the last bottle of liquor remained. One had already drunk himself into a doze in a chair in the corner, and the other two, without wasting any unnecessary words, were fast approaching that stage. Jerry was sitting on the floor with her head thrown back resting against the seat of a chair, and her co-hostess Marion was standing quietly looking out of the window.

They turned and looked when I came in. Marion stayed indifferently on at the window, but Jerry scrambled up and came over to me. "What happened?" she said in a low, amused voice. "Couldn't you get the money?"

"I got it, all right," I said ominously. "Where's Bernice?"

"She'll be right out," she said matter-of-factly. "I'll tell her you're here."

"Wait a minute," I said, catching her by the arm. "Tell me first—what went on? She—she waited for me, didn't she?"

Jerry screwed up her eyes and smiled at me indolently. I never saw her again after that night, but whenever I thought about her, I saw that lazy, murky smile she gave me then. "Oh, she got tired of *that* game," she said. "And a hundred years from now, it won't make a bit of difference, anyway."

I took her hand in both of mine and wrung it. "Oh, thanks, Jerry!" I whimpered. "You're swell! Now I feel like I was alive again."

But she kept on smiling, didn't stop smiling a minute, and all the way to the door she kept looking back over her shoulder at me, smiling, still smiling. "A precious little thing called love," I heard her say.

Marion came over to me then and said: "By the way! Does Bernice ever get any letters postmarked Detroit?"

"How should I know?" I shrugged. "I'm not her janitor."

"With handwriting like that of a ten-year-old kid?" she went on.

"What're you getting at, anyway?" I said gruffly.

"If you're ever sore at her," she persisted, "and you want to get her all scratched up by a girlie that knows how, just you pick up the phone and tell me you found a letter postmarked Detroit in her mailbox."

"Since when is the population of Detroit just one?" I wanted to know.

She turned around and stalked away again, as Bernice came out, followed by Jerry. My eyes lighted up as they found her, as though I had two batteries in my head for just such an occasion and, like a spotlight on a stage or like a lighthouse at sea, threw a halo around her to the exclusion of everyone, everything else, in the room. And every peach-colored flower on her dress seemed to glow back at me in the iridescent haze of love that drenched her. But she must have had an impalpable umbrella up, for she was as cool and arrogant as could be. "Well, Wade," she said, "back on the job again?"

I felt as though I had lost the Bernice I knew in the shuffle and was taking a stranger home.

"Good night, Marion," she called out politely, "and thank you for the swell party."

Marion never even turned her head, but her answer came at once, as though she had been plotting it for some time. "You're welcome," she said huskily, "and that goes for anything I've got. And if you're in touch with Sonny Boy at all, why, tell him I was asking for him."

Jerry, who had stayed behind at the door Bernice had just come through and seemed to be standing there listening carefully to something, raised a finger warningly and said, "You'd better go, Bernice. See you some more." So we walked out of the bungalow together.

While we were standing out on the roof waiting for the elevator, I heard a sound of hammering coming from inside. It was not very distinct, quite muffled. "Sounds like they're beginning to tap-dance again," I remarked. Bernice said, "No, that's some drunk who fell asleep in there; someone must have locked the door on him accidentally." But she moved around to the other

side of me and kept digging at the elevator door with her fin-
gernails before it was ready to open.

Bernice didn't say a word to me going down in the elevator,
which the indefatigable doorman had rendered habitable once
more, nor in the lobby either, although she turned and playfully
blew a kiss to his recumbent, inanimate form.

On the sidewalk she inhaled the fresh air, which the rain had
made cool and sweet, deeply and blissfully. "Wade," she said,
"have you got enough money for a taxi? I mean to ride around the
park in a couple of times? I'm afraid I can't go home just yet—
there might be some one still up at the place."

We got a taxi at the next corner, went up to Sixtieth, and
cut into the park from there. The gasoline fumes from all the
other cars doing the same thing that we were hung over the
trees like a diaphanous mantilla, and along every driveway stop-
lights were strung like a necklace of little red beads.

"Honey," I said, "what's the matter? Don't you own the place
you live in?"

"I do," she said, "Wade, but it's all mixed up—"

"Why should any one be there if you don't want them to?"

"I just furnish the background," she said. "They're having a
conference."

"Who is?" I asked.

"Nobody," she answered, and turned her head away.

I reached out and brought her hand over to me and kissed
the fingers one by one. "Bernice—" I started to say.

She turned her head my way again and said through
clenched teeth, "If you say one word about love to me right now,
if you put your hands anywhere near me, if I feel your breath
on my neck, I'm going to swing out with all the strength God
put in my arm and hit you so hard in the eye you'll never forget
it!" And she threw her head back, stared glassily up at the roof
of the cab, and moaned like a person in unbearable pain, "Oh,
God, how I hate love! I hate it, *hate* it!"

"What's the matter with you?" I asked alarmedly, "what are
you getting hysterical like this for?"

But I couldn't make her stop crying, panting through a shower of tears that she hated love, wanted to die, wished she hadn't been born.

The driver kept turning his head around anxiously, wondering what I was doing to her, I suppose. Finally, when I saw that I couldn't control her in any way, I asked him to take us out of the park by the nearest exit and stop at the first drugstore he came to.

When he did, I had him go in and bring her out a glassful of spirits of ammonia mixed with water, being afraid to let her sit in the cab alone if I went in myself and being unable to get her to come in with me, no matter how I coaxed.

When she was quiet once more, I had him take the empty glass back and I sat with my arm around her. "I'm not making love to you, Bernice. Just lean against my shoulder like this until you feel better."

"You're a good scout, Wade," she said, still shuddering a little from the sobbing.

I took a chance and said, "Wade loves you, anyway. You know that, don't you?" But the phobia or whatever it was had passed, and she just lay there quietly in my arms without attempting to "swing at my eye." Her knees were drawn up close to her body, and I covered them for her, and gave her form a little tug nearer me.

"I'm sorry I let it all out on you," she said, as the driver started the engine again. "If I hadn't been pawed to death the whole evening long, I wouldn't have gotten into a state like that."

"Do you want me to take you home now, Bernice?" I asked.

"Sure," she said with a melancholy air.

When I was paying the cab she said, "You can stay if you want, Wade. You don't mind using the living room for tonight, do you?"

"All right with me, honey," I said.

When we got, in the place looked as though a grand rehearsal of the Battle of the Marne had been staged there. Bernice acted as though she were used to finding it like that, or else she was too tired by what she had just been through to notice. Not a light had been lowered, not a thing put back where it belonged. The drinking glasses had been used for ashes, and the ashtrays for cuspidors. A heart-shaped taffeta pillow still bore the imprint of two heels, and a cigar stump that was now merely a cylinder of fine white ash had burned its way through one of the roses of the embroidered shawl and soldered itself to the varnish of the radio cabinet.

"Nice friends you have," I commented disgustedly.

"Friends?" she answered cynically. "What makes you think they're friends of mine?" She took off the little cap she had worn all along, sewn with little shiny things, and let it drop on the floor. Then she braced one foot behind the other, and pulled her heel out of her slipper, and when she had repeated the process with the second foot, she let both slippers stand there where they were and walked into the bedroom in her stockinged feet, tossing her little black silk evening bag at the seat of a chair as she went by.

I picked it up when she was gone and tucked it under my arm, and I took the hundred dollars out of my pocket and put it on the table, and looked around for an envelope. I found a yellow one with a little transparent "window" in it, belonging to a telegram that some one must have opened, lying on the floor, and I took a pencil out of my pocket and leaned over the table and wrote on it: "For you, Bernice, from Wade." Then I put the money in it and folded it over, and opened her little evening bag to put it in. But the marcasite button that I took to be the catch must have been just an ornament at the bottom of it, because while I was fooling with it trying to get it to work, the bag opened at the other end and emptied itself out on the floor. So I swore softly and got down on my knees and started to pick all her little things up: her lipstick and her key and her nail polish and her rabbit's foot and Lord knows what else. And four fifty-dollar bills, lying there like yellow autumn leaves. I put everything conscientiously back again and put my envelope in on top of it all, and then I closed the bag and went to the door of her bedroom with it. She had left the door ajar, but I rapped on the frame of the doorway without looking in at all. "What is it, Wade?" I heard her call from somewhere inside the room.

"Come out here and find out," I said shortly.

Presently the door slipped back, and she stood there looking at me.

"You left your bag out here," I said, and flicked my finger against it as though it were unfit to be touched.

"Oh, you could have left it th—" she started to say.

"Where'd you get the other two hundred from?" I lashed out at her.

"Why," she said with a peculiar smile, "don't you realize? You were gone a long time tonight."

I hit her with it in the face three times, back and forth and then back again, and then I let go of it and flung it at her, and it fell at her feet. She never moved, and as I turned my back to her, I thought I saw her nod her head ever so slightly, as though she understood, as though she agreed with me.

I walked out of the apartment and went out into the street once more. I remembered how I had nearly done this same thing the night I first met her, because she had insulted me about some ring or other she was wearing at the time. But this was different, this was forever, this was good-bye and be damned to you. There was no word for her any more in my vocabulary after what she had done tonight. You can cherish a loathsome toad, grow fond of a snake, tolerate a buzzard that feeds on the dead—but this!—oh, this was good-bye and never again. She had simply put herself beyond the pale. I stood on the street corner in the moonlight, I remember, and covered my eyes with my hands.

CHAPTER FOUR

"I came back to return your key to you," I said.

"That's very thoughtful of you," she said. "You could have left it downstairs with the doorman just as well, couldn't you? I happen to know you stopped by twice yesterday and once the day before—asking about the weather, I suppose."

I laid the key down on the table beside me.

"I wanted to be good and sure you got it yourself."

She sighed. "In the face, I suppose, like the pocketbook the other night."

"You got off easy," I told her. "I should have broken your arms for you."

"Houdini," she remarked to herself.

"No—just one of those that are born every minute."

"And since this seems to be the day for returning presents or what have you," she went on, "I have something for you, before I forget it." She opened a drawer and took out the folded telegram envelope I had put the money in three nights before. "Returned with thanks," she commented, and held it out to me.

I made a pass with my hand at it. "Give it to Tenacity."

"Tenacity gets paid good wages," she informed me dryly. "It's yours; you can't pull that millionaire-playboy stunt while you're wearing *that* kind of a suit—every time you turn around, I can see my reflection on the back of it." And stabbed the envelope toward me once again, less patiently than before.

"It isn't mine," I scowled ungraciously.

"You gave it to me, didn't you?" she told me.

"I gave it to you, all right," I said, "but if you must know, I held somebody up for it Saturday night, so either keep it or stuff it down the sink. I don't care what you do with it!"

She didn't say anything for such a long time, just looked at me, while I kept thinking: "Dumbbell! What'd you have to tell her that for? *Now* wait'll you hear the flock of insults she's getting ready to unload on you."

Finally she said in such a funny, quiet way: "Is that true, Wade?" I didn't answer. "Is that how you got that money? You did that for *me,* Wade?" And kept looking at me with eyes that weren't hard any more.

She spun the envelope away over her shoulder with a reckless sort of gesture, as though it wasn't important any more one way or the other, as though there was something else she wanted to talk about now. She came closer, and put her hands on my arms and shook me a little bit back and forth, just a very little, hardly noticeable bit.

"If I could only live up to *you,*" she said, "what a girl I'd be!"

I could feel little pinpoints of sweat coming out on my forehead, and I said, "Don't fool me anymore; you've fooled me so much—I can't *stand* it if you fool me anymore! It may be fun for you, but it's awful for me. It's inhuman and unkind. We should only suffer pain in dentists' chairs and on operating tables, Bernice, and not day and night, night and day, without a letup *ever.* It can't be done; it shouldn't be done."

She was the maternal Bernice this time; a madonna of tenderness and consolation. Oh, I found all things in her. She seemed older than me for a little while that afternoon; our profane love took on a semblance of sanctity. Her cheek was pressed to mine, cool, caressing, reassuring; our intertwined fingers were held before our faces in what unconsciously resembled an attitude of prayer. From the sky outside, the sun pierced the windowpanes and shot downward toward our feet in thin, golden tubes that were like the pipes of an organ. We neither of us moved, we each of us heard music and were fanned by benign wings.

"Bernice, Bernice, I'm not afraid any more. My love for you is stronger than anything you can do. That was the crisis, just past. Now it's immune, now nothing can affect it ever again; it goes right through to the end. So live as you've lived and do as you've done, and don't think twice about it—'cause *always, always,* from now on, you'll be right and I'll be wrong. And if you do things that seem strange to me or new to me, the error is mine, not yours. Just give me a moment's breathing spell each time, and then the strange won't be strange and the new will be customary. Vice and crime and all those other words—how do *I* know when to tack them on and when to leave them off? There's just you, and just me, and the rest is none of my business."

"My baby," she hummed, "my boy, my lover. I've loved you on and off now since I first began to really know you. Even Saturday night, when all that happened, I still loved you, Wade, I *still* loved you. In that room, up on that chair, I saw your face looking at me. Across the whole room I saw your face and no one else's; saw you trying to get near me, knew that I was torturing you—and yet, Wade, I *couldn't* get off that chair. No one made me get up there, no one would have stopped me from getting down. And yet I couldn't, I tell you, I couldn't! There was a scream way down inside me, a louder scream than all the noise in the room—oh, you would have heard it so clearly. "Wade! I *am* going to get down. Look! Watch! I *am* getting down." But it couldn't get to my lips, I couldn't bring it to my mouth. I didn't want to smile—and yet there I was braying with laughter. I didn't want to take my dress off—oh, *God,* I didn't want to after I saw your face—and yet I felt my own hands reach up to my shoulders and snap open the fasteners. Oh, Wade, are there two of us in each of us, a good and a bad—or what is it? What makes us do the very things we don't want to, know we shouldn't?"

We were silent for a long time, both of us. Almost it seemed as though we didn't have to speak to know what we were saying to each other. Then she went on: "The moment after you'd gone out the door, the moment after you couldn't see me any more, the moment that it was too late to ease your pain a little—I pulled up my dress around me like a flash of lightning, I got off that chair with a jump! Ask Jerry, ask Marion, ask anyone who was there what I said; they all heard me. I called out, 'All bets are off!' Some of them thought I was just trying to save face, I guess. One or two came up to me later on, on the sly, when they thought no one was looking, and tried to speak their pieces. I took a hundred dollars from the first one just as a joke and faked an appointment with him for the next evening, which I never kept. The second one followed me into another room when I went to get my things just before you came back. He took my pocketbook from me, opened it, and put the hundred in. He was drunk and couldn't keep his eyes open anymore, so when Jerry came to tell me you were there, I sneaked out and locked the door on him. That was the hammering you heard, remember? That's all there was to it," she said. "It was bad enough; but it wasn't as bad as it seemed."

I was convinced—that it wasn't true as she told it; that the true version was the one that had gnawed at my vitals for three whole days—from the moment I had found the money in her pocketbook until the moment I had come back here today. But how easy to forgive her when the lie was for my sake!

Or maybe this was the culminating irony of it all—that having believed her each and all of the many times that she was lying to me, when it didn't matter much to her whether I believed or not, now at last, when she was telling the truth and wanted to be believed (for there were tears in her eyes)—she failed utterly. I was inalterably convinced that she had lain with some one in that side room in Jerry's apartment.

But whether I believed her or not had nothing to do with my loving her; my love for her had now reached a stage where it could forgive anything she did. Only, perhaps, it was forgiving her once more than she needed to be forgiven.

"Other things, too," she said, "aren't as bad as they seem. Or maybe they're worse, but not in the same way. I know you know I'm not paying for the things I have here. You've known that because I've told you to be careful about phoning me, and all the rest. But you think I'm some one's mistress. You've never said it, but I know you've thought it all along, ever since the night you first set foot in here. Then get this: I'm not being kept by *one* man—I'm being kept by a clique. I'm not being kept because I'm loved—I'm being kept because I'm useful. I can't tell you any more than that. It isn't good if I talk. Bad for me, maybe bad for you too."

"Tell me you love me. That's all that matters, not who your friends are or what you've done."

We were sitting now on the divan in one another's arms, where one night I had found her handkerchief when I came in here alone, and where the other night that taffeta cushion had lain with the print of some one's heels bitten into it. "Wade," she said, "you complete the circle for me; by loving you, I've come around again to where I started from. Eight or nine years ago I used to go with a boy like you—*you* know, a boy who really loved me; it was only when I'd had the opportunity of comparing him to those that came later that I realized he must have been a pretty decent sort after all. Oh, he wouldn't have been healthy for a *good* girl to know—and yet when I told him I'd been drugged and kept locked up in a roadhouse overnight, he went out and got blind from wood alcohol. Since then I've been dragged through cage after cage of gorillas, and now once more I'm with some one who loves me. It seems so strange to hear those words 'I love you' and know they're really meant, really mine."

"They're no good," I said, "how can they tell you what I really want to say?"

"It's funny, it can't be explained," she murmured, "I feel sometimes as though you were sent my way to remind me now that it's too late; as though someone were shaking a finger at me and saying, 'See what you've missed, Bernice!' Oh, it's not *you* so much, honey, it's what you stand for in my mind; there's really nothing *to* you, you're just a man no different from a dozen, from a thousand, others—like that song that goes, 'Along came Bill, you'd see him on the street and never notice him at all.' But you love me for *myself,* that's what counts—and you're honest and you're not too cruel. The kind of girls that *get* your kind wouldn't understand me; they'd say, 'Who wants Bill? The world is full of Bills'; they're looking for romance, the saps, for sheiks and mysterious strangers. Wade, darling, I've had a man die in my arms—I've had to pretend to dance back to my table when I knew I was holding a corpse in my arms, so that people would think he was just drunk—with the blood coming out of the little holes where the bullets went in and soaking into my dress in spots the size of dimes. Maybe that's romance; to me it was just obeying instructions. They can have it; I want what *you* stand for. I want to take up *your* ways and drop my own. And it's just a little too late, I guess."

So the Plan was born then, as we sat there, and we talked it over ever so indefinitely at first, just skirmishing around the edges, afraid it would rise up and vanish like a mirage if we dared to look it too closely in the face. We were like two people bending over a pool of water and seeing our dreams in there, afraid to breathe on it for fear of causing a ripple. And what we said was set to the key of "If I had a million dollars" or "If I were the mayor of New York"; in other words, as though we both knew it could never be, but as though there were no harm in plotting and planning it just the same. Children often play that game: "If you could have just three wishes, what would they be?"

"—And if the worst came to the worst," Bernice said, "Lord knows, I'd have enough money to tide us over the first few months until you could find the right kind of job—"

"Oh, no," I said virtuously, "I wouldn't let you do that; whatever you have, you'd put away for yourself."

She drew her legs deliciously up under her and suddenly went down a notch or two lower on my arm. One additional little squirm of supreme comfort, and the game went on. "Let's see, now! I've got some rings and things in a safe-deposit box downtown—I haven't looked at it in years. I really ought to go down one of these days and find out just what's in it—I bet I could get enough on them to chip in with you on a car, some kind of a little Chevy, say."

"I've got a compound-interest account in a bank over in Brooklyn, it must come pretty close to three hundred by now. That would be so much to the good—"

"Wait a minute, don't interrupt," she said absorbedly, "I'm trying to remember things. Then there's that wristwatch with the platinum-and-diamond case—if I *were* going to do something like that with you, the first thing I'd do would be to get rid of all that junk; cold cash always is the handiest after all." She looked up over her head, and said, "Oh, God, I feel so happy this afternoon!"

I took her open hand and smeared it over my face. "Why don't we do it, Bernice? Why don't we do it? If it goes wrong, you could always take up again where you left off."

"No," she turned to me and said, "that's one of the main reasons why it's so out of the question. There'd be a lot more to it than just—changing over, if you want to call it that. To begin with, I'd have to get right out of New York. And I'd have to do it like *that!*" And she smacked her palms together and threw one arm up and the other down, like a person playing the cymbals. "I couldn't stay on here a minute once I did anything like that. Well, to speak quite plainly to you, Wade, I'd have to *duck*—and stay under cover for weeks, and maybe months."

"Why?" I said. "This is a big city."

"I've seen what happens too often," she assured me. "You wouldn't get *me* to stay here. Or come back within two years, either!"

"Well, okay, then we'd quit New York; it's not the only town in the country—"

"Believe me, we'd have to," she said doggedly, "it'd be either that or the observation ward at Bellevue for *me;* I wouldn't want to have kittens every time the doorbell rang while you were out."

"Ah, honey, that sounds sweet," I grinned. "One roof, four walls, and you and me!"

"And to be like other people are," she said, "and *love* each other, and to read the morning papers for the weather and the style hints and not—not for anything else. I'd give anything if a thing like that could only come true."

"It can," I said, "I tell you it can! Other people have made their lives to be what they want them to be. Why can't we? We're as good as any one else, and maybe a whole lot better; we've got that much coming to us at least! Ah, darling, don't back out; ah, honey, say it *can* be done."

She turned and flung her arms around me, and hid her face upon my shoulder. "It can't be done, Wade, can't be done!"

"Only because you don't want to; only because you don't think so!"

"It's not for me," she said. "Funny how you can go ahead as far as you like, but you can't take a step backward—*ever*."

"Only because you don't trust me; only because you're afraid—"

She stroked my face. "Wouldn't you be too—just a little—if you were in my place?"

"But Bernice," I protested, "what are you driving at all the time? What makes you always talk like this? What've you *done*? Is it the police you're afraid'll come after you—"

"The police?" she said with exquisite cynicism. "You mean those men in blue who stand in the middle of the street directing traffic all day long? Oh, yes, there *are* police—I'd forgotten about them for a minute or two."

"I can't make it out at all," I said dejectedly. "You talk in riddles."

"I *can't* say any more than I've said already," she protested. "I've tried to explain just where I stand! I've done more talking already than I have any business to be doing, for my own good."

"Yes, you always lead up to a certain point," I cried helplessly, "and then you stop dead and put me off with 'I *can't* say any more than that, don't ask me to explain.' It's happened over and over now. I've noticed it again and again. Why can't you come right out with it? What's always holding you back? I'm not just anybody at all to you any more, am I? It's all settled that we love each other, isn't it? Well then, why can't you give me the lowdown, the absolute goods, on what it is you're afraid of, on what you'd have to worry about if you left this place and came away with me? Who is it? What is it? Maybe I can help you. Don't you *trust* me? Are you afraid of *me,* too? Why won't you tell me?"

"All right, I'll let you have it, then!" she said. "Yes, I love you—and if you can't see that by now without my telling you, then maybe I've made a mistake in you altogether. But trust you?" She stopped and narrowed her eyes at me. "I don't trust anybody. I met you on the street; how do I know who sent you my way?"

"That's a *swell* thing to say to me," I said bitterly. "That's the swellest yet of all the swell things you've said to me since I've known you! Mud in my eye, all right! Every time I get through putting you all together, you fall apart again at my feet. Oh! what's going to become of us? Why, even everyday friends trust each other before love's even thought of. And you—and I—"

"I know the game from A to Z," she said meditatively, "and I know all the rules of it, too. And the one that should never be broken is—'Don't talk!' Love. Why, love is no guarantee! I've known people to have loved as much as we have, and known each other a darn sight longer, too—and before they're through, one has unintentionally done the other dirt—because they talked too much. And you—why, Wade, you almost love me too much for me to trust you; love and brains don't mix.

"All right," I said wearily, passing my hand at her, "that's forgiven, too, like all the rest. Have your own way; keep it to yourself. Maybe you're right not to tell me, and then again, maybe you'll find out some day it would have been a lot better if you had. But one thing's clearer than ever to my mind: you'll never be exactly as I'd like you to be until I can get you all to myself, away from whatever it is that's going on behind the scenes around here. Oh, won't you do it, Bernice? It felt as though we were so close to it a little while ago, and now we seem to have drifted away from it again, back where we always were."

"I want to more than you know," she said dreamily. "Let's do this: let's be happy with what we have, for a little while yet. Let's talk it over, and over, and over, whenever we're together and there's no one to hear us."

"But just talking about it won't get us anywhere," I whined.

"But just talking about it—that'll be something in itself. It'll be like selling the idea to ourselves, don't you see?" She glanced over at the clock, lit a cigarette, and called Tenacity into the room. "See if they left anything to eat in the Fridge, and bring us in a couple of little glasses of that Malaga, yes?" and turning to me when the other had left us alone again, whispered, "Don't say anything to me in front of *her*—ever, do you hear? She may be all right about little things, like sneaking off to a party, but beyond that—you never can tell."

I couldn't help wondering for a moment if she didn't have just a slight touch of the persecution complex, mistrusting everyone and anyone the way she seemed to. But kept it, of course, to myself.

"The first thing we'd have to think of," she said, "would be where we'd strike out for if we left New York together—" And then broke in upon the remark herself with the rueful observation: "But you see, I'm afraid we couldn't get enough together to take us very far."

"Well, how far would you suggest?" I asked with ill-concealed eagerness. "Buffalo? How does that strike you?"

"That wouldn't be a bit of good," she said instantly. "Not any large city in the east, nor any middle-sized one. That would be almost as bad as staying right on here in New York. No, it's got to be somewhere unexploited, like the Coast or New Orleans—"

"Unexploited?" I said blankly.

"Well, I mean—" she said, and didn't say what she meant.

"All right," I said happily, "then it's either the Coast or New Orleans."

"When the time comes," she reminded me quietly.

"Fair enough," I agreed. "When the time comes."

She said with elaborate dissimulation, as Tenacity came in carrying a tray. "What do you think they call gloves in German? Hand-shoes! Isn't that an uproar?"

"Where'd you dig that up?" I said, laughing at her rather than with her.

"Oh, I don't know," she admitted. "It just came to me this minute."

Tenacity was having a belly laugh over it; she left us hitting herself repeatedly in that region and bending low, cackling, "*Han'* shoes! Oh, shut me up! *Han'* shoes!" I expected momentarily to see her fall on her face.

"That'll be all over Harlem tonight," Bernice giggled. She turned to me and resumed: "Another thing: it mightn't be a bad idea if I started buying clothes now while the buying is still good, and get sort of a layout together. Even if nothing ever turns up, I'm that much ahead."

"What about the place here?" I asked. "I suppose there's a lease on it or something, isn't there?"

"I have nothing to do with that," she said, "I don't even know what I'm paying here. No, I'd leave everything just the way it stands, simply walk out the door as though I were going to the corner. That'd be the only way I could get away with it. I wouldn't even risk trying to get my trunks out; you see, they'd have to be expressed, and it'd be too easy to trace us through the labels. No, the day I *do* go, I'll just take a pair of good hefty valises right along with me in the cab to the station."

"Here's to that day," I said devoutly. "It can't come too soon!" And we clicked our glasses together.

"What you could do in the meantime," she suggested, "is scout around from this end and see if you can't get a line on some job or other out that way, so that when the day comes—"

"*Han'* shoes!" accompanied by a sputtering sound, was borne to us faintly from the bowels of the apartment.

"I'll stop in at the station when I leave here and find out what the tickets cost," I said, "so I can have that much laid aside ahead of time—"

"And what I want to do the first chance I get," she said, "is go down to that safe-deposit box and get cash for what I've got in there. I could go into some out-of-the-way jewelry shop with it, and if any one I know sees me, pretend I'm just looking at cheap necklaces or something."

"*Han'* shoes and *feet* shoes!"

"Oh, shut up," she remarked under her breath. "Maybe it'd be better if I passed it on to you and let you sell it for me," she added.

"I thought you said you didn't trust me," I said, trying to look injured.

"Oh, Wade, darling, I didn't mean in *that* way!" she cried remorsefully. "What I meant a little while ago was that there were some things I couldn't *tell* anybody, not even you, just as a matter of self-preservation." She got up and shoved the door closed with the tip of her shoe, just in time to silence another spasm of "*Han'* shoes!"

When I left, she came not only to the door, but crossed the corridor to the elevator door with me, and only the arrival of the car put a stop to our kisses. "Don't give our little scheme away to any one," she murmured low as the white signal light over us went out. "Gee, darling, didn't we have a happy afternoon!"

We flew back into one another's arms like two birds attacking each other in midair, and couldn't let go.

"When we're together we won't ever have to part."

"Gee, just think—'Frisco or Los Angeles, to call our lives our own!"

"I could be waiting for you like this and say, 'Come on in, Wade, the supper's waiting.' "

"You're the swellest thing ever happened in this world since Adam and Eve first found out what to do with their spare time."

"I only hope we're not two suckers," she said, "kidding ourselves along."

Tenacity stuck her head out and whispered, "They're asking for you on the wire—"

"Wake me up, I've been dreaming," Bernice smiled at me sadly as she went in and closed the door. I went down in the elevator.

Home like a bullet, and the wheels as they ground around under me did nothing but sing, "Some day soon now, some day soon." I almost missed my station, listening to that encouraging song, but a last-minute bolt from the strap I had been standing under got me out of the car just as the doors were closing. When I came up on the street again, the light had changed color, as though the sun had put a lot of rouge on before going down for the evening. Shadows were mauve on the sidewalk, and the world had a carnival air.

I opened our door, and Maxine came to meet me from a chair she had placed to one side of the window, which had enabled her to look down without being seen from below. "What was she doing that for?" I wondered vaguely.

She seemed to have one of her quiet moods on. "What was doing?" she asked me, without kissing me.

"What do you mean, what was doing?"

"I mean, how are things getting on?" she said.

"Oh, no different from any other time," I said offhandedly.

"Did you see Stewart today?" she asked then.

"He's there all the time," I replied, opening *The Sun.*

"I didn't ask you that, Wade," she insisted. "I asked you if you *saw* him today, if you spoke to him."

"What's this all about, anyway!" I shouted suddenly. "I'm trying to read something in here—and you—"

She sat down opposite me and folded her hands in her lap, the very picture of docility. "I knew you'd lie to me," she murmured.

So I let the paper toboggan to my feet and gave her my undivided attention, at last. "Come again?" I said politely.

"*I'm* the one would like to know what this is all about," she told me dejectedly, "not you. *I* don't want to row with you; you know I don't. But *why* do you pretend to me you were at the office today, when you know you weren't? You don't think that makes it any easier for me, do you?"

"Makes what any easier for you?" I said embarrassedly.

"They called up today and wanted to know why you weren't there. I suppose now you'll blame *me* for it. If you'd've told me ahead of time, I would've gladly fibbed for you and told them you were sick or something. But I was so taken back myself, I didn't know what to answer. They said you weren't there all day yesterday, and the day before you only came in for a minute and went right out again without saying anything—" She stopped for breath. I needed some too, although I hadn't been saying a blessed word. "And they said for the past few weeks now this has been going on steadily, you've stayed away without any explanation at all, at the rate of once every two or three days. They said they're not going to stand for it any more." She turned her eyes away from me at this point, as though she was the one to be ashamed, not I. "Wade, you've lost your job."

I gave a convulsive little start. "Did they say that too?"

"Imagine how I felt," she went on, "hearing a thing like that over the phone, from some one I'd never seen before in my life! I said, 'I'm sure he can explain; haven't you spoken to him about it?' They told me they were sure you could explain too, but that they weren't really interested any more in hearing what you had to say; and would I please tell you when you came in that your check was being mailed to you at the close of business today, and you'd get it by the first mail in the morning. And then who-ever it was had the cheek to say to me, 'He *does* come home sometimes, doesn't he, ma'am?' and I heard him snicker to him-self. I've been crying all afternoon," she concluded in a barely audible voice.

"Their bark is worse than their bite," I remarked after a proper interval of meditation. "I'll stop in tomorrow morning and talk to Stewart, hear what he says about it. And if not, there are plenty of other jobs. Don't let it break your heart." And thought to myself, "What's the difference if I'm canned now? I would have chucked it over myself anyway in a month or two more—whenever *she's* ready. It's all to the good—and I can make up the difference in money in one way or another between now and then." What I really was pondering in those few minutes was what to tell Maxine I had been doing with my time when I wasn't at the office.

"It's too bad it had to happen," she mused. "You've been staying out on me at nights often enough lately, but I never thought you'd go this far and let your work go hang."

"It *is* too bad," I agreed sociably, "but it's done now, so what's the good of talking about it."

"Of course, as a mere wife," she said, "I don't suppose I have any right to ask what you were doing with yourself when you weren't at the office. Any more," she added ironically, "than I had any right to ask what you were doing with yourself the several nights that you didn't sleep at home lately. We'll let that go; sufficient unto the day is the evil therefore."

"Thereof," I corrected learnedly.

"Well, this isn't a schoolroom."

"Oh, no? Well, that's what it's felt like to me for the past half-hour."

"Too bad," she commented. "Poor abused man!"

"For God's sake," I said, "stop fidgeting with the bottom of your skirt, will you! Can't you keep your hands quiet? I'm so nervous I could jump through the ceiling!"

"Wade," she said, "have you been seeing some one? Who is it you've been seeing? 'Cause I know you haven't got many men friends, *they* wouldn't take up so much of your time—"

I thought of the previous Saturday, and answered, "I know I haven't; I found that out too."

"You don't want to answer," she said to herself, and had a gust of crying and sobbing.

I waited until she was good and through, then I said: "Are you all through now? Good! Well, since your heart's so set on checking-up on me, I'll tell you exactly how I spent yesterday and the day before—"

She turned and gave me a look as though she was afraid of what I was going to say next, almost would rather not hear it. But I noticed that she didn't stop me from going ahead, just the same.

So then I gave her an elaborate, ironically elaborate résumé covering the eight working hours of those two days, sixteen hours in all. Not a detail was overlooked; I took her with me step by step on those long, aimless, tortured walks I had taken, back and forth across the town, that resembled so closely a distracted man pacing to and fro in a room. And when I interrupted myself to recall that I had had an orange juice at Fifty-Fourth Street and Broadway, or that I had bought *The Sun* at the downstairs stand in the Pennsylvania subway station, she didn't dare resent the irony implied in my giving her such details. The account was exhaustive; exhaustive and exhausting. I almost mentioned each time I had sought a washroom. Three incidents, and only three, were not exposed to her: my one interrogation of Bernice's doorman on Monday and my two repetitions of it on Tuesday.

But, womanlike, she still seemed dissatisfied when I was through, seemed to be looking for a motive in all this. As though I had overreached myself in giving her more details than were necessary and yet at the same time withholding the key to the situation. "But *why* couldn't you stand the thought of sticking in the office all day? *Why* were you so distracted? What was the matter with you? You haven't told me that yet. What was on your mind? What made you chase all over town like a chicken with its head cut off, without knowing where you were going at all?"

"I don't know," I said, "couldn't tell you if I tried. And that's that. Take it or leave it. *I'm* no psychologist."

"And was it the same thing with you today?"

"Identically," I said shortly.

Then she began to lean toward credulity. "Wade, maybe you've been working too hard. I'm worried about you. Maybe you should see a doctor—"

"And maybe I should see the Golden Gate with my Bernice," I thought feelingly.

"Mrs. Greenbaum told me that after they have the fur sales in August her husband always gets in such a state he has to go to Bear Mountain for a week—"

"With some blonde, I bet," I said aloud.

"He's not that kind of a man," she pouted. "They're a very devoted couple—"

At which precise moment, as though they had only been waiting for a signal from us to begin, a sound of angered footsteps crossed our ceiling, and words of dispute came crackling through sections of the fragile plaster, now here, now there. "You should be such a man like he is!" And then over in the other corner, "You should live so long—I'm too good for you!" It was timed too perfectly; it was unreal. It was not life, it was the movies. And yet it happened.

Maxine made no attempt to save her face in the matter; her laughter mingled unabashedly with mine. We rocked uncontrollably on our chairs and looked into each other's eyes to add fuel to our enjoyment of the situation.

"They live like *doves!*" came from over the chandelier. I could see the chandelier throbbing from the force of this statement.

For a moment I even harbored the delightful suspicion that we were the couple in question, but it seemed not. "Believe me, Sadie don't know how lucky she is! I'll tell her the next time I see her—!"

"Tell her a thing or two about yourself, why don't you, ha?"

I noticed, however, in spite of this last, that the repartee or whatever you might call it was predominantly feminine. Perhaps Mr. Greenbaum *was* a devoted man after all. Or else his wife's voice carried much better through laths and plaster.

When we were both completely laughed out, and the situation had begun not only to abate but to pall as well, Maxine leaned confidentially forward in her chair and said to me, "Wade, darling, I was so upset about what happened this afternoon, I didn't get a thing in for tonight. If I get my hat and coat, will you take me out to a restaurant? We haven't done that in such a long time," she added coaxingly. "Will you, Wade?"

"Sure," I said generously, touching her cheek with one finger, "why not?"

When she had come running back with her things on and preceded me out the door, I remarked, "But no postmortems, do you hear?"

She looked around at me tenderly over her shoulder. "I'm sorry I was mean to you, Wade," she said. "It'll all come out all right, won't it?"

I was too busy locking the door to answer.

By the very next morning, which was Thursday, I had already begun to get up later, now that I didn't have to be in on time any more. We had breakfast at ten, and Maxine rather seemed to enjoy the idea than otherwise. The peace, well-being, and even amiability that had descended upon us following the Greenbaum explosion the evening before persisted in the sunlight of the breakfast nook. Maxine's green curtains looked cozy, and I had a paper there I had stepped out to buy while she was getting the coffee ready. It was all okay; I mean as a temporary vacuum to tide me over until Paradise began with Bernice, it would do very nicely.

I finished the paper and she the dishes at about the same time. The check from my late concern had come, and I had it in my pocket; I had told her a little earlier that I didn't think I would go back and cringe to Stewart just for the sake of getting the job back, that this had pulled me out of the rut I'd been in all along, if nothing else, and I preferred to go out and get a newer, more lucrative job, even if it took me a week or two to find what I wanted. Which is not altogether the empty boast it may sound; jobs were plentiful and times were good.

I got up from the table, stretched, yawned, and said, "I think I'll blow now."

"I wanted to go downtown too today," she told me. "They're selling out those little collar-and-cuff sets at Gimbel's; I need one for my dark blue." Which didn't interest me at all. I didn't even know what she meant by her dark blue—probably one of her dresses.

"If you'll wait till I put something on," she went on, "we could ride in together." She was still in her pajamas.

"All right," I said, "how long will it take you?"

"I won't be five minutes," she promised, and went into the bedroom.

When eight of the five were up, she came out again fully dressed to tell me: "Wade, what do you think? I just found a hole in the heel in one of my stockings!" This calamity leaving me unmoved, she went on: "Maybe you'd better go ahead; I have another pair drying over the steam pipe in the bathroom, but they're still a little too damp to put on."

"I'll go ahead," I decided, "and meet you down there later. Whereabouts you going to be?"

"You can wait for me in front of Gray's Drugstore," she said.

"Make it about one," I told her, "we can run into the State or the Rialto and take in a show before they jack the prices up."

"Fine!" she agreed. "I'll be through by that time."

"And see that you make it one," I warned her as I opened the door, "and not three or four!"

"I'll be there," she sang.

I got off at Times Square and shuttled over to Grand Central first of all, and went up to the ticket office in the station to find out what the fare to the Coast came to roughly. Roughly was right, too; I nearly fell over when he told me. "Is that *one* person?" I gasped. "I didn't say a caravan," he answered tartly. "She was right when she said we ought to be sure of what we're doing ahead of time," I told myself despondently. "You're blocking the window," the ticket seller reminded me, so I asked him about New Orleans. That was pretty nearly as bad, but then, when I left the window, I looked at a relief map they had hanging up on the wall and found out that New Orleans wasn't nearly as far away, so it seemed a much better buy and more of a bargain to pick California when the time came to leave. Also,

I didn't know much about New Orleans, but I knew that all kinds of flowers and fruits grew in California, and so it seemed to me to be the place to start life with the one you love.

As I walked west along 42nd Street, I was figuring with a pencil on the back of an envelope, and I kept bumping into people at every step. I went into the Automat and had a ghost of a lunch, and all the time I was in there kept figuring; when the back of the envelope was all used up, I started in to use the shiny, white top of the table, until a busboy with a greasy rag came along and, whether accidentally or on purpose, effaced the whole thing with a sweep of his arm.

When the dispute had died down and every one had gone back to their seats again, I started over again, this time using the margin of a newspaper I'd picked up from the floor. I started in to mumble to myself, like the old, the feebleminded, and the preoccupied do. "Three-hundred-and-some-odd would make it six hundred, roughly, for the two of us. Now let's see, without counting what I've got in the Corn Exchange—I don't want to touch that if I can help it; leave it here for Maxine, that's the least I can do, even if she hasn't got a kid—nearly three hundred in that compound-interest account over in Brooklyn—and if I put in that check for eighty I got today, that'll bring it up to four hundred by the time I'm ready to go. That leaves me two hundred short, even on the fare alone. Wait! I can borrow two hundred on my insurance, that does it! But that leaves me without anything when we get off the train there—and I don't want Bernice to help me in any way."

The interested stare of my table companion, who was getting an earful while he dipped little round crackers in clam chowder, put an end to the soliloquy. I left the place and continued westward toward my appointment with Maxine, still calculating as I went, except when crossing streets. "All right," I argued with myself, "suppose Maxine *is* a good kid and *has* given me eight years of her life, why should I give her a better break than the girl I love? I'll take half of that Corn Exchange account with me, or *all* if I have to, and send it back to her as soon as I start to make some money out there. It won't put her out much anyway; she can stay on in the flat rent free the first month after I'm gone, on the deposit we paid on the lease. And she's got her stepbrother and his wife, they'll do something for her if worst comes to worst. So that takes care of that, and all I have to do now is bide my time and keep a good crease in my trousers for the day we leave!" I threw the newspaper away, brushed my hands hygienically (it hadn't belonged to me originally), and backed up against the glass-window front of Gray's Drugstore to wait for Maxine. It was five to one on the Paramount clock across the way.

Swarms of people, principally women, were going in and out the door, buying theater tickets at the cut-rate counter and keeping their appointments on the sidewalk outside, like I was. I thought, "Maybe I ought to get out of the way instead of standing here like this. Suppose Bernice should just happen to come along and bump into me, and Maxine should find me talking to her!" But I'd never seen Bernice on the street after the night we'd first met, and there was no reason why I ever should again. "She's only just about getting out of bed by now, anyway," I assured myself.

With that, a taxi edged up to the sidewalk, stopped in front of the entrance to Gray's, and a girl got out of it alone and paid it off. She turned around then, and it seemed to me I'd seen her somewhere before. But you so often feel that way about people. She was dark-haired and she was handsome. I don't mean beautiful, I mean handsome; there's a difference.

She was still putting the change the driver had given her back in her purse, but she looked up to make sure no one was about to collide with her—and saw me. She took a second look— then she finished putting the money away, snapped her handbag shut, came across the sidewalk, and stopped in front of me. At first I thought she was looking at the display of cosmetics in the window behind me, but I saw that her eyes were right on mine.

"What's the matter, can't you say hello?" she said in a husky voice. The clock on the Paramount said one.

"Hello," I said obediently, and still at a loss.

"You don't remember me, do you?" she said unfriendly. "You ought to, you drank enough of my liquor the other night!"

"What makes you think I don't remember you?" I said uneasily.

She took her eyes off me at last and looked sullenly up the street and then down the street. "Well, the name's Marion," she said.

It was no pæan of joy to my cars. "Well, I knew that all along," I said. "So what? What about it?"

She turned her eyes on mine again. "Still in good with Bernice?" she wanted to know.

"Bigger and better than ever," I answered shortly, and then as a hint, "Going to a show?" The clock over there said four after, now. I was praying she'd go away. What'd she want with me anyway?

"She gotten any mail from Detroit lately?" she wanted to know.

"Who, Bernice?" I said. "Why should I tell you that?"

She flashed me a dark look and said: "Oh, I guess she has, if that's the case. Just let me find that out! Just let me find that out!"

Because I didn't like her anyway, and because she was annoying and worrying me by standing there like that when I expected Maxine to show up momentarily, I revenged myself by teasing her and telling her what I thought would be most likely to get her angry. And at the same time rid me of her. "She gets 'em from Detroit at the rate of two and three a week, sometimes," I informed her amusedly. And then, remembering something she had said the other night, added, "*You* know, funny scrawly handwriting, like a little kid at school."

I could see that made her angry enough to eat the glass window we were standing in front of. "And you stand for that!" she snarled. "What kind of a guy *are* you?"

"What's the harm?" I said smilingly, "he's in Detroit."

She finally prepared to depart, although by the stony look in her eyes it appeared doubtful to me whether she could see where she was going at all.

"You better run along to your show and cool off," I advised her jocularly.

"Show be damned!" she rasped, and darted into a taxi that someone had just gotten out of. Through the door I saw her lean forward and say something to the driver; he put on the gas and turned up 43rd Street, and that was the last of her.

I kept smirking to myself for a long while afterward at the state of mind I'd managed to get her into.

Meanwhile Maxine didn't put in appearance, and the afternoon prices went on at all the picture houses. It was too late now to go to a show and still be economical. Presently, as the hands of the clock circled slowly around, I was nearly as angry as my late acquaintance had been. All the theatergoers had gone from the scene long ago. At quarter to three, wondering if perhaps she had never come downtown at all today, I went inside and phoned home to the apartment. Sure enough, she came to the phone herself. "Wade?" she said noncommittally.

"Well, who'd you think it was!" I burst out maniacally. "Mayor Walker?"

As though she were thinking about something else entirely, she repeated evenly after me, "No, I didn't think it was Mayor Walker."

"Why didn't you tell me before I left that you weren't coming downtown today, instead of making me hold down the street corner for two solid hours waiting for you like a goddam fool!" I shouted at her.

"I *was* downtown, and then I came home again," she said quietly.

"What was the bright idea of doing *that?* Didn't you remember you had an appointment with me? Couldn't you at least have gone past here and told me you were going home? What am I supposed to be, anyway, a flagpole sitter?" And more along the same lines.

Finally she said, "Oh, what do *I* care? I'm standing here dazed, I can hardly hear what you're saying at all. I'm going to hang up; you better tell me first whether you're coming home or not."

"You talk like you were drunk," I said to her.

"I wish I was," she answered. "That'd be *something,* anyway."

"What's the matter, don't you feel well?" I asked solicitously.

I heard her say to herself: "He asks me whether I feel well!" and then she *did* hang up. I immediately tried to get her back again, but she wouldn't answer the operator's calls.

So I gave up and took the subway home, wondering what had got into her *now.* "I know it hasn't anything to do with *me,* this time," I reasoned on the way back. "Maybe somebody she knows just died; why couldn't she have told me over the phone just now? Or maybe she's going down with the flu— That'd be a real treat; doctor bills at a time like this, when I'm trying to hang on to every cent I've got!"

I couldn't wait until I got up the steps again, those subway steps that I seemed to spend so much of my life going up and down; and over to the place, and in the door. I could've saved my breath and energy: she was as well as I was. Not only that, she looked much better than she did at other times. Sartorially, if not physically. For she had on full makeup instead of just half makeup or none at all. And she had a pair of her 1920-model glass prisms dangling below her ears. And a dress that I associated vaguely with the words, "Oh, I can't wear that; it's too good!" And perfume escaped from her at all angles, although rather faintly, as though it had been doing so for a considerable number of hours now. All in all, her getup denoted that she aimed, or *had* aimed, to please and charm.

For a moment I even misled myself to the extent of thinking that I might be the object of her pleasure-giving efforts, or whatever you want to call them. But she hadn't met me as she had promised, and somehow I had an idea that all this finery dated from earlier in the day. I knew darn well she hadn't put it on just to greet me when I came home. Only a year ago, and I would have been open to jealousy at a juncture like this. Worrying, wondering if she had been seeing someone. The time for that was gone, though, now. She could have done what she wanted. What would I have cared any more?

"Boy, you look classy!" I remarked cordially, sticking my thumbs into my vest pockets and studying her with my elbows akimbo.

"I tried to make myself look that way today," she said dully. "I meant to change when I got back here, and then I forgot to, I guess."

"You act all down-in-the-mouth, though," I remarked. "What was the matter with you over the phone just now? Why didn't you show up today?"

"Sit down," she said indifferently, brushing my questions aside with a limp drop of her wrist, as though they were of no moment at all. "I have something I want to talk to you about."

Not her appearance but still her attitude, even the very way she had just seated herself sidewise on the chair and rested her forearm and her chin along the back of it, suggested a gin-soaked old scrubwoman to me. One of those old crones tired out with life and chronically stewed to the gills.

I wondered if thirty or forty years from now she was really going to wind up that way, the way she had just now struck me as seeming for a moment. I wouldn't know her any more in those still-far-off days, and she wouldn't know me any more, but too bad if it had to happen: the little flapper I had danced the Japanese Sandman with eight years ago! She had been the youthful of the youthful—

She began to speak.

"I went to see her today. And, honey, she was *nice*. I expected her to laugh at me, I expected her to make me eat dirt. And, honey, she was *nice*. Honey, you won't believe me, but she was *nice* to me—"

I could feel my eyes growing bigger.

"—real *nice* to me. Honey, you'll only laugh, I know, but we *cried* together, me for her and she—she for herself, I guess. But I *mustn't* lose you. Honey, I *mustn't* lose you."

"Who?" I panted. "Who?"

"*You.* Who else? *You.*" She tried to stretch out her arms toward me. I pushed them aside. "No, *who?* Who were you with?" I could hardly talk with my windpipe all closed up.

"Bernice," she said. And as I heard the name on her lips for the first time, but spoken so casually, as though shock or grief had turned all values upside down for her and made a name like that seem like an everyday household name to her ears, I simply sat back; I was beyond surprise, regret, humiliation, or anger. "Here," I remember thinking, "is either an unusually wonderful person, whom I have no longer the wish nor the time to understand, or the biggest dumbbell in the world, who doesn't deserve any better than she's going to get."

She smiled ruefully and said, "I wish I had worn that stocking that had the little hole in it, and left when *you* did this morning. I mightn't have ever found out. But I guess it's better that I know about it—" And looked at me almost as though expecting me to confirm her judgment in this. "That taxi driver came to the door a little while after you'd gone—*you* know, the one you promised to pay—and he said you knew where his stand was but you'd never come near him to pay him since that night, and he said he wasn't going to wait any more, he'd come here to collect. I had quite an argument with him and told him he was drunk and—oh, what's the use going into it? He didn't *purposely* tell me anything, but the few things he let drop fitted in so well with what I knew already—about your staying away from me all the time and getting in wrong at the office and walking around so crazy all day yesterday and the day before— so I thought maybe it would do some good if I—had a talk with her, just had a talk with her—and at least find out what I was up against or what was going to happen to me. I found out from him where it was, and I tried to make myself look as pleasing as I could, and—" She gave a pathetic little shrug. "I drank a tablespoonful of your gin and went there—"

"Wasn't *I* the one to talk to? What's *she* got to do with it? What do you mean by dragging *her* in it for? All right! You'll see how much you gained by it, you'll see what good it does you!"

"It did this much good, anyway," she said humbly, "whatever happens now, I know *she* won't be to blame and I know *I* won't—it'll be all up to you, Wade."

"You're telling me," I said ungraciously. And sneered. "Now just what was it you said to her makes you so sure of that? Let's have it!"

"Oh, I didn't walk in there like they do in the movies and say, 'Give my back my husband!' Why, Wade, Bernice didn't know you were married! I *know* she didn't. Leaving me out of it altogether, I wouldn't even call that fair to her her*self*—"

"What do you think you are, a court of justice?" I demanded resentfully. "Did *she* complain about it? Did *she* say she's got a kick coming?"

"No, all she said was, 'That may surprise *you* in a man, Maxine, but it doesn't me any more.' "

"I notice you got pretty chummy, calling each other by your first names," I said enviously. "What'd you do, sign a blood pact together? Too bad you didn't both keep on bleeding a while longer!" It made me almost as furious at Bernice as at Maxine herself to think they had gotten on so well together—especially without my being there. I suppose, subconsciously, it would have suited the male in me much better to know that they had clawed and scratched each other's eyes out over me.

"I almost like Bernice, in spite of everything," Maxine mused. "I suppose a lot of women would call me crazy—because, after all, she's stepped in where she has no right to—but I don't blame *her* for that, not one bit. If I were single and had been through all she's been through—"

"Single!" I thought to myself bitterly, "around the noon hour each day, and that's about all!"

She looked at me a very long time, just sat there and looked at me like a calf looking at a man with a butcher knife in his hand. I didn't speak either; what was there to say? Then she began to make her plea, the big plea that she must have been preparing all afternoon. It wasn't very eloquent; but eloquent or otherwise, what chance did it have with me?

"What was in your mind all the time, Wade? You weren't thinking of anything—anything *permanent,* were you? You mustn't. It'll blow over—"

"Will it?" I thought, and didn't answer.

"We've had so much fun together, Wade. Even when we've fought it's almost been like fun—compared to—compared to *this.* Fun to sulk, and fun to make up. Do you remember the time we got so sore at each other on the train, and we each swore we'd have separate rooms when we got there? And then, when we *got* to Atlantic City, there was only one double room left in the whole hotel? And we had that big screen brought in and put up between us? And it fell over in the middle of the night? And we were each of us sitting in exactly the same position, on the sides of our beds with our hands around our knees, listening? Wade, darling, we were like lovers in a musical show in those days. Boy-husband and child-wife. Let's carry the thing through. Let's sing our duet, kiss and make up. Let's not throw it all away. It's here with us now. Why should you, why should I, begin all over with somebody else?"

"All right, can all the chatter," I said brutally. "I'd much rather hear what the upshot of it all was this afternoon. I suppose you drank tea and ate ladyfingers together! And then what? What was the final word when you left?"

"Why, nothing," she said, "what *could* we say? I wasn't going to make a fool of myself and ask her not to see you any more; what would be the sense of such a thing? You're the only one can decide *that,* Wade. Which is exactly how she feels about it herself. 'I'm the passive party in this,' she told me, 'it's something that'll have to be settled between you two. You go home and talk to *him* about it,' she said when I left, 'and more power to you—' "

"Traitor!" I thought poignantly.

" '—and if you can get him to look at it your way,' she said, 'why, tell him to give me a ring and let me know, that's all. *I'll* understand.' "

"Hypocrite!" I fumed inwardly. "I'd like to kiss all the lies away from your lips, I'd like to kiss you and punch you for that until you squeal!"

"So there it is," she concluded with a dismal sigh, "and here we are."

"I don't know what you expect me to say," I answered crisply.

"Say what you mean," she said. "Say just exactly what you feel like saying. God knows, no one's trying to bully you!"

"Thanks!" I laughed coldly.

"You don't need to hide anything from me, either, Wade. I know just how far this thing's gone."

"What kind of women are there in this world today, anyway!" I exclaimed disgustedly, throwing my cigarette deliberately on the floor and flattening it with my foot, then kicking it away.

"Oh, she didn't have to tell me *that,*" Maxine answered with equal disgust. "Don't you suppose I can *tell?*"

"Good!" I said with feigned briskness. "Then you know the worst!"

"It isn't *that!*" she tried to tell me. "Oh, Wade, Wade, don't you understand it isn't that! Weeks ago, already, when you stayed out like you did, I *felt* there was something doing—only I thought maybe it was some drifter you'd picked up in a speakeasy or on the street and then never seen again afterwards. Every married woman has that happen to her at some time or another. But this—this isn't as disrespectful to me, maybe, but it's a whole lot more dangerous. *That's* what I'm driving at, *that's* what I'm trying to get out of you—what do you intend doing? Is it going on like this, or what? You surely must have known I'd find out at one time or another; you didn't expect to be able to lead a double life under my very nose indefinitely, did you?"

"Double life!" I mimicked. "Don't be so dramatic, will you?"

"Dramatic is good!" she laughed bitterly. "I'm supposed to sit back and not say a word while everything I've got goes up the flue. Maybe *you* would if it happened to you!"

"Ah, baloney!" I said.

She stepped into the bedroom a minute to get a fresh hand-kerchief. "Better bring a few of 'em with you," I called after her. "No telling *how* long this thing's liable to keep up."

She came back holding the new handkerchief over the lower part of her face. "Even ten-year-old schoolboys know enough not to hit a fellow when he's down," she said through it, her watery eyes peering at me above it.

"Cut out the martyr stuff," I advised her. "That won't help any."

To my surprise, she did immediately, and became coldly disdainful.

"Nothing would with you," she said. "You're not worth my letting you see me cry over you. And if I feel like crying over you when you're not around, I suppose that's my tough luck."

"Good!" I said to myself, "maybe she's going to get sore; then I'll have an excuse to walk out of here."

She didn't say anything for a while after that; just sat staring out of the window at nothing. Then, after fully ten minutes, she turned around and remarked, "You must be hungry, Wade. Why don't you run down to the corner and get yourself something to eat? I haven't got anything here for you."

"What about you?" I said, standing up immediately. "Get your hat and come on."

She looked at me pityingly. "I'm not a man," she said. "I couldn't eat right now—or any time tonight. You go ahead—"

At the door I said, "Want me to bring you back some sandwiches?"

"No, thanks, Wade," she said, "but do you want to—"

"Do I want to—what?"

"Do you want to kiss me?"

I went over to her, bent over her, and felt her lips reach up to mine.

When I got to the door a second time, I remarked, "I'll be right back."

"That's up to you, Wade," she told me.

I didn't pull the door smartly enough to after me, and it slipped back and stayed on a crack, so after I'd punched the button for the elevator, I stepped back to it to close it more firmly, and glancing through into our living room, saw her in there with her head buried in her arms on the sill before her, crying soundlessly to herself. I felt mean about it for a while afterward, but I couldn't see what there was to do about it even if I had felt inclined to do something about it. "She ought to save her tears," I told myself, "she's going to need them a few months from now."

I went into a lunchroom near where we lived, collected far more unsavory dishes than were necessary on a tin tray, and sat myself down at a table to eat and think it over, commingling the two processes without any difficulty on account of being, as Maxine had said, a man.

Bernice's attitude occupied me principally. Had she really meant that when she said that if Maxine could persuade me into not seeing any more of her, it was all right with *her?* "She *couldn't* have really meant it," I assured myself. "She can't *possibly* be that indifferent if she's ready and willing to throw everything over and go away with me!" But the gruesome thought kept presenting itself: "Suppose she's just been stringing you along, taking you for a sleigh ride, as they say; suppose she *never* intended to go away with you from the beginning, and that's why she's so complacent about Maxine putting the crusher on you if she can?" It was all I could do to keep away from the telephone and sound her out on it then and there. But something told me it would be wiser not to ring her up right on top of Maxine's visit that afternoon. "She may be sore about it; it may have riled her a little, even if she didn't let on to Maxine. And you never can tell about women—she may take it all out on me, if I ring her up right now. Better if we both sleep over it; better if I wait till tomorrow." And I consoled myself in this wise: Bernice hadn't let a word drop about our intentions to Maxine, she had confined the discussion (from what Maxine told me) to what had gone on between us in the past few weeks;

didn't that argue that she had been acting a part to bluff Maxine, that she had no idea of relinquishing our scheme of going off together? I felt that it did, and felt a whole lot better about it than I had at any time since the bad news had broken two or three hours before.

"I'll make it my business to see her tomorrow," I said, slipping spoonfuls of rice pudding and raisins in and out of my mouth with relentless accuracy, "and I bet I'll find out I'm right!"

Maxine was in bed when I went back, and though I felt sure she wasn't asleep, her eyes were closed, so I didn't speak to her. I noticed a little shiny thing, like a pearl, under one of her eyelids when I put the light on. A tear, I guess.

CHAPTER FIVE

I didn't bother phoning Bernice the next day but went right up there to see her a little before two. I felt unusually cheerful, as though Maxine's visit and the revelation of the day before had cleared the air for all parties concerned. It didn't feel as though I were double-crossing her any more to come up here—although I hadn't told her that I was going to, just the same.

"Hello, hand-shoes," I greeted Tenacity, "is my lady in?"

Tenacity said she was eating her lunch, and when Bernice wanted to know who it was through the door, called back with unreproved familiarity, "Wade!"

She was sitting at her vanity table when I went in, or whatever you call those low things with triple mirrors and no drawers of any kind under them, and had all her beautification implements pushed aside to make room for a little tray containing a cucumber sandwich and a glass of frothy pink stuff that I took to be a strawberry soda. She pointed the second cucumber sandwich toward me, not offering it to me but indicating me by it, and waiting until she had finished chewing and had swallowed, remarked: "I *thought* you'd be around today!" At the same time, there was a mischievous, bantering light in her eyes that boded well.

"Sit down," she said, pointing the sandwich at a chaise lounge. "Be through in a minute. I never do this, but I didn't have any breakfast this morning."

I had made up my mind before coming not to say anything to her until she had mentioned the subject first. About Maxine's visit, I mean. Because, for all she knew, Maxine mightn't have even told me and I might still be in the dark about it, so I wanted to hear what she had to say first. Therefore I made casual conversation while she bit her way busily through the second sandwich and sucked up the pink stuff through two straws.

"Gee, it's a pipe of a day today, gold dust 'round your feet. You shoulda been out hours ago. What was the matter, hangover from last night?"

"No," she said, "I simply overslept. Tenacity never wakes me, you know, and for the first time since I've been living in this place, the phone didn't ring once all morning! Don't know what to put it to. I even had her call the operator and have it tested, I was so sure it must be out of order. Nothing the matter with it, just an off-day for me, I guess." This while she bent her head forward over the tray and the pinkish stuff drew together at the bottom of the glass and then was gone. "Not that it worries *me;* some relief, let me tell you. 'Jever try answering a phone with your eyes closed and a lot of cobwebs over your mouth?" She threw her arms back over her chair and stretched, turning her wrists out, then in again and beat them idly together. "And I never yet got in the tub but what I got a call and had to hop out again. Didn't seem like a bath at all today. Light me one too." She straightened up in her chair once more, tumbled her hair over her eyes, and blew smoke through it. She looked like a haystack beginning to catch fire. "By the way," she said, turning half-around toward me, "I don't know whether you know it or not, I had a visitor yesterday." And her eyes crinkled mischievously at me.

Here it comes, I told myself; let's have it! And let's hear what really went on between the two of them.

"What's the catch?" I said innocently. "That's no event in *your* young life, is it?"

"Wade," she smiled, shaking a finger at me, "you've been holding out on me."

"*I* have? What do you mean?"

"You see, in Europe," she laughed, "the married men wear rings just like the women do. It has its advantages."

"What's it all about, Bernice?" I said genially. "Let me in on it."

She reached across, picked up my hand, and looked at it ostentatiously, turning it this way and that. "Tell the truth, Wade," she said then, cocking her brows at me, "are you married?"

"Yes, sure I am," I said readily. "Why?"

"You wouldn't fool a girl, would you?"

"I wouldn't fool a girl like you."

"Well, do you think that's nice?" she asked. "Why didn't you tell me that all along?"

I knew all this was just byplay. " 'Cause you didn't ask me," I said.

"We'll let that go," she laughed. "Anyway, your wife was here to see me yesterday."

"All right, I'm listening."

She glanced over my shoulder. "Close the door," she murmured.

When I had returned to the chaise longue once more, she went on, "Say, Charlie, my boy, does it take a stick of dynamite to jar *you,* or didn't you quite get what I just said to you?"

"You say Maxine was here to see you," I said, enjoying myself hugely.

"Yes, *Maxine,*" she said. "And let me tell you she's a darn nice kid, too."

I made a face. "You can have her."

"I don't want her," she said, but she was a little more serious now, "and how would you like it if I told you I don't want *you* either?"

"Not very well," I admitted, "so don't."

"She's a damn nice kid, Wade," and there was no mistaking the fact that she had stopped being playful. "I don't see *how* you've got the heart to do anything like that to her; it would be an awfully low trick."

I sat up tensely all at once. "What would?"

"Leave her in the soup like that."

"You mean, what we've been thinking—what we've been figuring on? Bernice, you're kidding me! you're not going to leave me flat *now,* are you?"

She pointed her cigarette right at my heart, and it was as though she held a long spear in her hand instead of a Chesterfield when I heard what she was saying. "*Get* me, my used-to-be. I'm not bighearted. Maxine isn't worrying me a bit; it's myself that's worrying me. Do you think I'd take a chance on you after the way I see you're ready to sidetrack her? Not me! Why, it wouldn't be eight months, instead of eight years, before you'd pull the same thing on me. She's got the law on her side, and I wouldn't even have that—nothing but my hips until the day you got tired of them—"

My face, I guess, was all gray by this time. "Bernice, darling, you don't know what you're saying. *Don't,* will you! Don't go back on me! Always, always, it's because you don't *trust*— won't *trust!* Haven't you even got confidence in the one that loves you? Won't you give human nature the benefit of the doubt one time out of a hundred? Can't you see, as a *woman,* that you've got me where you want me, that I'll eat out of your hand until the end of my days? What *more* do you want? Have I stopped for a minute and thought that you might fall for some good-looking guy when we're on the Coast, and leave me flat if he happened to be able to offer you more than I could? And isn't that much more likely to happen? Oh, Bernice, if I can trust *you,*" I groaned, "with the odds against you the way they are, *why* can't you trust me just a little, honey?"

"No soap," she said inflexibly. "I'd rather hurt you now than get hurt myself later. Hold yourself together a minute; just stop and look at it my way. I'm supposed to throw over everything I have, everything I'll *ever* have as far as I know, and make tracks with you. Which isn't a mere nothing in itself, no matter which way you look at it. But *wait!* there's more to it. If I do that, I'm quitting a game that *can't* be quit. Do you understand, *can't* be quit. Do you want to know what that means? That I'm *marked.* No explanations accepted. The day I walk out of here with my arm on yours and my satchel in my hand, there's no turning back. I can't show my face anywhere in the east from that day on. I'd be *marked,* I tell you. And if you don't happen to know what I mean by that—I mean out of bounds, marked for the ax." She let that sink in for a minute, though as usual I thought she was exaggerating to impress me, and was too wrought-up myself to pay much attention anyway. "And what do I do it for?" she went on. "What do I get for it? What's the percentage? So that a year from now, maybe, I can wait on tables in a West Coast cafeteria? Or show Filipinos how to fox-trot? I guess not!"

"So you think I'd do that to you," I said miserably. "So you think that's the kind I am."

"I'm not sure you would," she said, "but I'm not sure enough you wouldn't, either, to make the thing a safe bet as far as I'm concerned. No, Maxine was a godsend, she snapped me out of it in time. I'll wait a little while longer before I cut my own throat."

"So you're dead sure that we're through?" I answered.

"Have I said a word about our being through?" she corrected. "Do I act as though I was ready to give you up? No— what's through and *out* is this idea of our going away together. That's off the list; I'm playing safe, that's all. But that doesn't change the way I feel toward you. It *couldn't.* The only thing is we'll have to go on the way we are, I can't see any other way. I'll stick around here and take my orders from the phone, the way I—"

"Oh, *yeah?*" I said furiously. "You dope things out pretty much to suit yourself, don't you! This is *out,* and that *goes,* and heigh-ho the merry-o! Well, you've got another guess coming. It's all or nothing, now. *I* can't go on like this, sneaking in your back door all the time, suffering the tortures of hell when I'm not with you. I lost my job this week on account of you. Either we clear out together like we planned to all along—or else we're through once and for all; it's good-bye, starting in right now! Is that plain enough?"

I leaped up from the chaise longue with a brave show of willpower and stood looking at her. "You heard me! Which is it going to be—yes or no?"

She tried to put a restraining hand on my coat sleeve. "Now, wait a minute! Don't get all hot and both—"

"Wait, nothing!" I exclaimed, brushing her hand off. "You've kibitzed around with me long enough. You're driving me mad! Are you coming away with me like we planned—or aren't you? That's all I want to know, that's all you've got to tell me."

"You know where I stand," she said surlily, breathing on her nails and brushing them against her palm. "Do I have to repeat? I just got through telling you!"

"Good-bye," I said bitterly. "I'm through. I'll get you out of my head if I have to kill myself!"

"You'll come back," she said, still polishing her nails and not even looking up. "This isn't the first time you've pulled this stunt on me—"

I got to the door, the room door; I even got it open. Oh, I could have gone on down to the street. I could have gone quite away and stayed away a day or two whole days, like when I found the money in her handbag. But in the end, didn't it all amount to the same thing—the door, the street, a day, two days, and then I'd be back again. Sure I'd be back. Or I wasn't Wade, and she wasn't Bernice.

So I shortened the whole process by turning back right then and there, right where I stood, at the door of her room, and dropping back on the chaise longue that was still warm from me just now, turned my back to her and sobbed hotly into my cupped hands.

Having gained her point, she could afford to be magnanimous, was over beside me then in no time at all, down on her knees with her arms knotted around my neck, drawing my face down to hers again and again. "Men don't cry," she remonstrated gently.

"It's all right, Bernice," I said after awhile, "don't feel sorry for me. It'll be all the same to me from now on; I've just gone down for the third time."

"Wade, I love you so. And New York isn't the worst town there is. We'll have such swell times together! Let's let the rest of it go hang. We'll see each other all the time. And by each living under separate roofs, we'll be that much better off—we won't have a chance to get tired of each other like we would the other way—"

"You're right," I told her submissively. "You're always right. I told you once you were always right—"

She left me only to go to the door and open it, and then was back again beside me. "Tenacity!" And when the mahogany face had poked its way in, "Fix us up a couple of long ones. Long and strong. We're having a celebration in here."

And while the trip westward, and the bungalow on some sunny Los Angeles street, and the Chevrolet, and all the rest of it faded slowly away like the sun was fading outside the windows, she lighted my cigarettes for me between her lips, had the radio going softly, kept passing her hand over my face as though she wanted to learn its outline by heart, and made it seem to me that I had given up nothing and gained everything in having her near me like this, having her love me like this. What more could any one want?

Tenacity brought in two more "long ones" without being told to, around four o'clock. She looked at us, shook her head sympathetically, and carried the empty glasses out with her.

Bernice tasted hers, and blew her breath out as though to cool her mouth. "They're strong, all right. It's funny, I can never trust her to do my mixing for me."

"But you told her to make 'em strong," I reminded her.

"Yes, that was to begin with, but you should taper them off—she ought to know that by now. I guess the reason I notice it so," she said, putting her glass down, "is, these are the first drinks I've had all week. And today's Friday."

"We had some wine together when I was up here Wednesday," I recalled.

"Yes, but not hard drinks. I haven't had a hard one since the night we were up at Jerry's and Marion's. Let's see, that was last Saturday. That'll be a week ago tomorrow."

"Oh, by the way," I said. "I forgot to tell you. I ran into Marion yesterday, outside of Gray's Drugstore."

"Jerry with her?" she asked idly.

"No, she was alone; she was going to a show, I think. She stopped a minute and spoke to me. I couldn't remember for the life of me who she—"

She picked up her glass again and went ahead with it where she had left off, remarking, "She's the sweetheart of one of the big shots here in town. She's in pretty thick with—well, all sorts of people that I know."

"All I know is, she's completely sold out on some guy in Detroit called Sonny Boy," I laughed.

"Not so loud," she warned me, half-jokingly, but with a glance at the door. "It isn't good to know him anymore. One time he was a big shot here himself. Then he ran away to Detroit. Now he's on the outs with the New York crowd—"

"And jealous as all hell," I went on, contemplating the contents of my glass. "Always asking me if you're getting letters from him in Detroit." I took a long drink. "I didn't know how else to get rid of her," I resumed, "so I kidded the life out of her, told her sure, two and three times a week regularly. She got so sore, she couldn't see straight, didn't even go to her show—"

Over the rim of my glass I happened to raise my eyes to her; I couldn't understand, lowered it out of the way in a hurry. The lap and the whole front of the pale-violet satin kimono she had on went deep purple all at once with the puddle of liquor soaking into it. The glass glanced off her kneecap, bounced clear of the chaise longue, and sang out from the floor, miraculously unbroken. But it was her face, her *face!* A mask of white fright pulled taut from ear to ear, where her prettiness had been only a second ago; then slowly relaxing again, like elastic, into a more recognizable semblance of her. Her eyes had been unbearable for a minute, the pupils rolling insanely upward and disappearing under the upper lids. They came down again and stared hauntedly out at me. And her voice, when she found it, was furry as with an inner strangulation.

"You've signed my death warrant!" she rasped.

"Bernice!" I cried in alarm. "What is it? Here, swallow some of this—!" But as I passed my glass toward her, she shot up from where she had been sitting and ran halfway across the room toward the door, then stopped abruptly and looked dazedly all about her, as though not knowing which way to turn. I was terribly frightened myself by now, not knowing what to make of it, thinking she must have either gone temporarily insane or else was undergoing a sudden spasm of violent physical illness. It was awful to see the way she clutched herself through the satin kimono, now on the arms, now under the ribs, as though at a loss what to do next. I caught her in my arms where she stood finally—for she brought to mind a pathetic little trapped animal that wouldn't let any one near it—and forced almost all the liquor I had left in my glass down her throat. She gagged and retched on it, but it brought her back a little, brought a smarting moisture to her eyes and dimmed that berserk look they'd had in them for a minute or two.

"God, what a fright you gave me!" I said, clinging to her.

"Oh," she kept moaning, "they'll get me for it! They'll get me for it! My time is up, all right! That was the *one* thing you shouldn't have said—"

"Wait a minute," I said, "until I call Tenacity—maybe she can help me with you."

"No, no, no!" she exclaimed, "don't let her in here—!"

I led her back to the chaise longue and seated her on it by main force. She clung with one hand to my sleeve, as though afraid I would leave her, and with the other kept pounding me lightly on the chest, distractedly emphasizing what she was saying. "Oh, what am I going to do, Wade? Help me! What am I going to do? They're going to get me as sure as you're born! She was the last one you should have told that to—my God, if it had only been Jerry, any one else—but *Marion!* She's in thick with the big muck-a-mucks; it'll get back to them in no time—!"

"But Bernice, darling!" I pleaded. "I was only kidding her along. If it's not true, what can she do to you, what are you so afraid about—"

"What *can't* she do!" she gasped. "One word from her, and—she's the sweetie of—oh, don't you understand? What chance have *I* got! She won't come up here and try to pull my hair—if that was all there would be to it, I'd gladly lie down flat on my back and let her kick my teeth out. She'll let *one* word drop where it'll do the most good and—do you think they'll let me explain? I *know* too much; they won't take any chances!"

I tried to soothe her by stroking the backs of her hands; she drew them away from me suddenly and cried: "I wish I'd never known you! After I've watched my step so carefully all these years, *you* have to come along—and get me in a spot!"

"It's as much your fault as mine," I defended myself. "If I had *known* what was what, if I had *known* who I was talking to there on the street! I sat in this very room with you only the day before yesterday," I reminded her, "and *told* you it might be a whole lot better if you let me in on what you were up against, gave me some idea. But no, you couldn't *trust* me, had to keep everything dark—well, it sure worked out beautiful *your* way. Maybe next time you'll have a little more confi—"

"*Next* time?" she cried, jumping up again. "There *isn't* any next time in this for me, don't you understand! That's why I'm so cokey over the whole thing! Wait!" she said, running her hand along the side of her face and on up through her hair. "I've just got one chance left! If she hasn't spoken to anybody yet, maybe I can square myself with her. But if she's already given 'way on me, then there's nothing left to be done. I'm washed out! Tenacity!" she shouted wildly, "Tenacity! Come in here, damn it!"

Tenacity appeared in the doorway with remarkable abruptness, in fact almost instantaneously, as though she had been listening to the whole tantrum from beginning to end. The scared look on her face was a perfect match for ours.

"Quick! Get Jerry's place on the phone for me—the number's on the pad there. I'm too excited to find it! I want to talk to Marion Scalero. Nobody else."

"I don't have to find it. I know the number of Jerry's place," the awestricken Tenacity said.

"Well, *get* it for me; don't stand there, you fool!" Bernice barked.

Tenacity collapsed onto the telephone bench as though she had had a heart attack and picked up the instrument with trembling fingers. "Marion Scalero, understand!" Bernice reminded her, and to me, wringing her hands in an agony of impatience, "She can have anything I've got! Oh, if I can only get around her in some way—!"

Tenacity having stated her number, we both held our breaths, listening and waiting. Bernice edged closer to her, ready to take the instrument from her.

Suddenly Tenacity put the phone down and turned to Bernice. "Their number's been disconnected."

She stamped her foot. "Don't tell me that! It can't be! We were up there only Saturday—"

"That's what the chief operator just said to me," Tenacity insisted.

"They may have moved out since then," I observed.

"Look in the directory under apartment houses," she instructed Tenacity exasperatedly, "and call up the building they live in; maybe they can tell us what's happened. Only hurry it up, will you, hurry it up!"

I strolled over to the window meanwhile and started to look idly down into the street. "Keep away from there!" Bernice said to me sharply. "Don't show yourself at the window, you never can tell who's watching!"

I withdrew leisurely, a little bored with all this melodrama, and went into the serving pantry to get some more gin and vermouth, which it seemed to me she needed more than she ever had in all the time I had known her. I came back, holding one in each hand, just in time to hear Tenacity saying, "They were dispossessed Monday morning on account of all the noise up there Sa'day night; they didn't leave any address with the superintendent."

Bernice literally snorted with dismay and began to screw up her face once more into that horrible mask of panic. "Here, try this," I quickly forestalled her, afraid she was going to lose her head again. She drank, sketchily and drippingly, and brushing her hand quickly past her lips, said: "Wade, there's only one thing left for me to do now—" And giving me a meaning glance, she turned to look at Tenacity. "Wait a minute, don't say anything!" she murmured.

Tenacity was still sitting at the telephone, staring from one to the other of us with her thick lips dropping open.

"You can go home now, you're through for today," Bernice said to her briskly. And throwing open a drawer, she took out some money and put it in her hand without counting it.

Dismay burst its way through Tenacity's opaque features. "Ain't you gonna need me no more?" she piped thinly.

"Oh, sure, you come back about nine in the morning, like you always do," Bernice assured her hypocritically. "This is just so I won't forget what I owe you. Now hurry up and go, will you!" And she actually went to the door and held it open for her, impatience expressed in every line of her body.

Tenacity got to her feet, moved across the room toward the door, and through it—and was instantly effaced by the shutting of the panel, which Bernice effected almost before her skirts were out of the way. *"Now!"* she exhaled, leaning her back against the door for a moment as though to gather fresh energy from it.

"What's the one thing you said was left for you to do?" I asked eagerly, going to her. I already knew, though—something told me.

"I'm going with you, if you'll still let me," she said.

"My baby!" I cried gleefully.

She caught at my shoulders and shook me anxiously. "Can you do it, though? Can you *make* it? It's got to be right away—not next week, not even tomorrow. I've got to get out of here by tonight, I tell you!"

"It's a cinch, nothing to it!" I said elatedly. "There's a train for Chicago at about nine-thirty, and we can take the Santa Fé from there tomorrow morning—"

She began to pull dresses out of a closet, then stopped to throw off her violet satin kimono right before me. "No time for modesty right now!" she gasped. "When was it you say you saw her—yesterday?"

"About one in the afternoon."

"Well, the damage's been done long ago—there's not a minute to lose—if I want to see thirty!

"Wade, *do* something, will you!" she cried, in the act of twisting a dress that had just dropped over her shoulders this way and that around her waist. "Don't stand there watching me—do you think I'm kidding you, or what?"

"Well, I'm waiting for *you*," I said. "We'll leave here together."

"How *can* we?" she wailed, snapping a row of little hooks closed over her ribs with the agility of someone playing a musical instrument. "I've got to throw some things into a valise, and it's twenty-five to five *now!* The banks closed an hour and a half ago—and you'll need some money, won't you! What are you going to do?"

"Gee, you're right!" I yelled. "I never thought of that! I can get in if the manager's still there—otherwise I'm sunk!" And I bolted for the door. "I'll pick you up here in less than an hour."

"No, don't come back!" she called after me. "I'll meet you at the station at train time. I'll be through before you most likely, and I don't want to wait alone here in the apartment. But for God's sake, see that you get there!"

"Grand Central—lower level—eight-thirty or quarter to nine!" I babbled wildly, half tearing the door from its hinges.

In the foyer I was fleetingly aware of Tenacity's presence in the background, standing before the mirror pretending to put on her hat or something. "Mister Wade," she said querulously, "is Miss Bernice fixing to fire me, or what—?"

"Look it up in the almanac," I said roughly, and was gone.

I jumped into the first taxi I came across—this was no time to count pennies—and made a beeline for the Corn Exchange, *my* branch. It *would* be much further away from where Bernice lived than two or three of the other branches!

I had no time to be happy that we were going away together at long last; there was too much to do first. I could be happy later on, on the train. But how glad I was (I told myself) that she was high-strung, neurotic, or whatever you want to call it, and imagined all sorts of dreadful things would happen to her if she stayed in New York after I made no more than a casual remark to some girl who was somebody's sweetie; how lucky for me. Otherwise I never would have got her to go with me. Too vivid an imagination and perhaps too much liquor and too little sleep over too long a period of time had accomplished what no amount of love and devotion could have.

But at the moment there were other things I was just as glad about, too. I was glad I had struck up an acquaintance with that insipid trombonist in the jazz band at the Pier the first summer Maxine and I were down in Atlantic City seven years ago, never dreaming that he would outgrow his insipidity, discard his trombone with his white flannel trousers, and become first a teller in a bank and then the manager of that bank—or at least, of the branch I dealt with. Otherwise, what chance would I have had of withdrawing money from a three-o'clock bank at quarter to five in the afternoon?

When we got there, the doors were closed, but I rang the bell and motioned frantically to the watchman through the glass. He motioned back to me that the bank was closed (as though I didn't know that!), that it was too late, to go away, or something to that effect.

I thought I was sunk for a minute, and felt myself beginning to wobble, like a concertina left standing on end. But I
went back to motioning again, with the added device of shout-
ing through the glass and getting it all misty with my hot
breath.

He finally indicated a side entrance, met me there, unlocked
it, and thrust his head out.

"Mr. Plattner go home yet?" I demanded breathlessly. If he
had, curtains!

"Who are you?" he said.

I gave him the name and said, "Ask him if I can come in
and speak to him for a minute."

He locked up, went away, stayed away, came back, and unlocked once more.

"We gotta be careful, these days, y'know," he said, by way
of invitation to enter.

I found Fred in his office, the whole place very solemn-
looking under green-shaded lights. I'd come in like this after-
hours once or twice before, but that was because we were going
to have dinner together or something. And that had been the
first year he had the job, not lately. But at least my barging in
now wasn't an utter innovation. "Hello, Wade," he said, shaking hands with me across a glass desktop. "Where *you* been
keeping yourself all these years?"

I didn't tell him that, but instead I told him I wanted to close
out my account.

"Kind of late in the day, isn't it?" he mentioned. "Tomorrow
suit you just as well?"

"I'm taking the nine-thirty train to Chicago with my bundle
of happiness," I told him, "and I haven't a nickel in my pocket."

"Oh, you're taking Maxine with you?" he said interestedly.

"Maxine doesn't spell happiness for me any more," I told
him point-blank. "Do this thing for me, will you, Fred?" And I
said to myself: "If he gets moral all of a sudden and tries to talk
to me like a father, I'm gonna throw the inkwell right in his
eye—even if I get held up for damages!"

But he didn't say a word, just looked at me attentively for a minute, then asked me if I had my passbook with me, and told me to write out a check for the full amount. I had the check written almost before he was through speaking, but I told him I didn't have my passbook with me. They had a duplicate there, though, so that didn't make much difference; he told me to mail the other one in the first chance I got. He okayed the check, and then I thought I might as well kill two birds with one stone, so I showed him the other one I'd gotten from my late firm earlier in the week, which luckily I hadn't deposited yet over in Brooklyn as I had planned to, and he okayed that too. Then he shook hands with me, wished me a lot of luck, and said, "Let me hear from you some day, Wade."

I went outside to the cashier's window and cashed the two checks—the cashier still being there, fortunately, and being occupied in separating dollar bills that had gotten wrinkled from dollar bills that hadn't gotten wrinkled, or something like that. The watchman let me out the side entrance, and I found my taxi driver pacing back and forth, aged with worry and impatience. I looked at the bank clock through the window—it was just five, to the minute. As long as I wasn't going to meet Bernice until eight-thirty, there seemed to be no reason why I should ride all the way home in a taxi when the subway "gets you there just as quickly too." So I paid him off and bade him Godspeed—or the modern equivalent of it, which is a fifty-cent tip.

I went over to the station next and got the tickets—which made the wad of money I'd gotten at the bank much less conspicuous to carry around with me. I glanced across to the other side of the big, vaulted place, echoing with hundreds of footsteps all at one time, and picking out a certain spot under a light, said:

"There's where she'll be standing three hours from now. I can see her *now,* so neat, so sweet, so all-around complete, with her big valise beside her on the ground and one little foot pointed out ahead of the other. Waiting for *me,* lucky stiff!" And I tipped my hat to the empty place against the wall and half closed my eyes for a minute, with reverence and ecstasy.

I realized there was no chance of getting at the compound-interest account I had over in Brooklyn any more; even if the bank had been open, you have to take a blood test and let yourself be fingerprinted to get money out of one of those accounts. So there was nothing left to do now but go home. I wasn't going home because I wanted to say good-bye to Maxine—I could've done that over the telephone from here just as well. I was going because I wasn't in awe of her enough to go all the way to California without my shirts and socks and handkerchiefs. And since there was still nearly three hours' time left and nothing else to do, why not go home, take a bird's-eye inventory of my things, and pack a grip? I got on the subway and went.

In the act of putting the key in the door, I stopped and looked down at it, held in the flat of my hand. "Last time I'll be using it," I said thoughtfully. "I'll take it off the ring on my way out and leave it in the door." I opened the door and went in.

Maxine wasn't in yet. "The breaks!" I chuckled to myself. "I can get all my packing done calmly and systematically, without having her yell blue murder over my left shoulder all the while."

So I dropped my hat over the telephone, stripped off my coat and vest and draped them over a chair, and rubbed my hands briskly together in token of anticipation. Then I took a minute off to turn the radio on, and as I left it, I was unconsciously mimicking the brazen noises it gave out. "Shouldn't," I reproved myself, and stopped. "I'm leaving her tonight."

I went into the bedroom, and the evening sun made the walls of it look like the inside of a wicker box that has been full of crushed strawberries. I threw open all the drawers of the bureau one after the other—bang! slap! bang!—and then I pulled my valise out of the closet and opened it on the floor. I hadn't used it since the last trip to Atlantic City, the summer before. There was still an old bathing shirt rolled up in the corner of it. I got it out of the way and flung it unceremoniously into a far corner.

Then I began to pile shirts in like one of those three-decker sandwiches, colored ones on bottom and on top and white ones in the middle, where they wouldn't get dirty so quickly. When the shirt angle was through, my other suit came to mind—at the dry cleaner's, two blocks away. *The* other suit. "Too bad," I sighed. "Have to get a new one out there; I'm not going out after it now any more, save my strength for the trip."

The socks I packed last, after everything else had gone in, because I knew by experience they could be rolled up in balls and wedged far down into the corners of the thing. The neckties I left out altogether, because there was no way of folding them or anything, and they kept sticking out all over like thirsty tongues each time I shut the lid down on them. So I tossed them all back where they came from. "Get new ones," I said recklessly. "Starting a new life, so I'll get everything new to match it!" I locked the valise at last and stood it up against the wall, where I wouldn't trip over it. Then I pushed all the drawers back in again, and tried not to look at Maxine's silky, fluffy things, left all to themselves now that mine were gone.

It was quarter to six by the time I was through, and she hadn't come yet. "Wouldn't it be just like a movie show," I thought grimly, "if she didn't get back on time and I had to leave her a note!"

And ridiculous, fantastic, or insane as it may sound, I found myself growing actually impatient and fretful over her lateness, as though my going away depended upon her being there to say good-bye to. "Just *tonight* she has to be late!" I caught myself saying with a scowl. "Every other night she's always around here hours before I get home! I suppose she's standing chewing the rag over the counter with the A and P manager's wife—"

It never occurred to me to make my getaway bag and all, now that the coast was clear. Because somehow I didn't look upon this as *deserting* her. It was almost as though I was too proud of my love for Bernice, thought too much of it, to *sneak* off without a word.

I looked at myself in the glass and, with that immemorial gesture of the hand on the chin, decided that a shave wouldn't hurt me any. Although tonight wouldn't be the first night that I was with Bernice, Lord knows, still, with every passing minute I felt more and more like a young lover ready to start off on his honeymoon. Anxious to make a good appearance, giddy with love and the attainment of an ideal, impatient, deliciously nervous, shivery like a person about to dive from a height into unknown water—I was even a little shy and diffident at the thought of facing her, as I never had been before now.

I stripped off my tie and shirt preparatory to shaving. At which point the door opened, and Maxine at last came home. "You there, Wade?" she called the length of the apartment. That, it occurred to me, was a needless question; the busily vibrating radio should have told her *someone* was home, and there were only two of us, so it must be me. Most women talk before they think.

"Yeh," I said curtly.

"I had the *worst* time getting spaghetti," she said, still from a distance.

"Don't tell me they're running short of cans!" I said hopefully.

"Every one had that kind with the cheese and tomato," she continued absorbedly. "I had to walk *blocks* before I came across the kind you like, with the mushrooms."

"I suppose I ought to feel bad, now," I told myself unwillingly, "now that she's put herself out to get something I like the last night I'm with her." I had decided long ago that I was going to eat at home.

"I'll be ready for you in a minute, now," she promised, still trumpeting her remarks from the kitchen.

"No hurry," I assured her. "I'm going to shave first."

"Oh!" she called back disappointedly, "do it *after*ward, Wade, there won't be time; I've put the can in the water already."

But it would have taken more than a mysterious symbol of speech like that to deter me from making myself presentable for the woman I was wild about. I went ahead in the bathroom.

CHAPTER SIX

I stood there in a cubicle of white tiles that gleamed like milk, and my shoulder blades, still shiny from the dregs of last year's tan, caught the light like copper epaulettes. Beyond that there was not much to me; a man who stood and carefully scraped his check and rinsed the blade under the faucet and was thinking: Bernice! . . . Bernice! . . . Bernice! For there had never been anything to me at all until now, but now there was this to me: that I loved her. And that made it all understandable to me; my being born, my swallowing certain quantities of food each day, my aimless roaming from one room to the next, out one door, in the other. I was given my body, and for twenty-odd years all I could find to do with it was put underwear on it once a day, park it in an enamel tub now and then, shove it in a bed at night and let the life slip out of it. I was given my hands, and the most they could do was make that little upward curve and down again, striking a match to a cigarette, when they should have been, oh, should have been, around her waist all the time. I was given my voice, and all I ever used it for was to say things like "Scramble two and a cup of Java" to Swedish waitresses, and "What are we waiting for, come on, let's get married and get it out of our systems" to poor Maxine, with my heart in cold storage all the time. But now all this was changed; now I got a break at last. Now rooms were not empty and food was not sawdust. Now body, hands, and voice knew what to do. Now *she* had appeared on the scene at last. The fog had lifted and a star shone through; now all was clear to me at last. And was I glad I hadn't given up too soon! Was I glad I hadn't ever tried to do a leap off some bridge with bricks in my pocket! Was I glad I hadn't patronized strange bootleggers! Was I glad I'd still been in short pants in 1918, and was I glad I'd let that gunman have that ten-dollar bill without a word of protest under the Sixth Avenue L that night! Was I glad I'd lasted till I met her, never knowing she was on the way!

Now I was pressing my face between the two ends of a towel. Then I pushed open a little gadget on the stopper of a powder flask, and five little pinpricks appeared where there hadn't been any before. A few white grains dropped out of each pinprick when I shook, and onto my face to turn into complexion. I was through now, and I poked at the wall, and the lights fled. And with them went the gleam like milk, and the bathroom had turned blue all around me. Blue, that badge of the nineteen-twenties. A hundred years ago it was just a color; today it was a mood, the soul of a generation.

Maxine came to the door and rested her palm high up against it, near the top. She clutched a dishcloth in her other hand; there was something pathetic about her in that loincloth she called a dress, reaching from her armpits to her hips, with a little rubberized apron across the front.

"Be right with you," I remarked absently, and passed by her and went into the bedroom. I heard her turn around and go away again. "I'm not going to call you any more," she warned me. But I didn't even turn my head.

I plunged my hand into a drawer that was like a nest of vivid tropical snakes. Neckties. And finally pulled out a dark-blue one with little green spearheads set far apart. I shut the drawer and never saw the rest of them again after that night. When I had tied it, I put out the lights and went in to her.

She was already seated at the table, and though one part of her would have liked very much for my food to be cold and unpalatable now that I had kept her waiting, the other part of her that wanted me to be happy no matter what the cost had made her put the dishes back on top of the stove and cover them over. She herself had already begun to eat, but she jumped up and got my portion from the stove as I sat down. Our heads were both slightly bent, as though we were two children not quite sure of our table manners as yet.

I looked at the plate before me, and my mind told my hand to take a fork and put food in my mouth, but my stomach told my hand not to, so I lit a cigarette instead.

"What's the matter, aren't you hungry?" Maxine said.

"Sure I am," I lied to her, "just give me time. Don't rush me, see?" And if she pulled that old reliable one beginning: "After I went to all the trouble of cooking—" I knew I would hit her. But fortunately something distracted her attention just then, and the matter of food was allowed to drop. Above us, there was a flourish vaguely resembling music, and then the radio began to articulate one of Kern's pieces from *Sweet Adeline.* A moment later the one under us had joined in and was whinnying forth the same number. "Wait a minute, I must get this!" Maxine cried, jumping up from the table, and turned on our own instrument in the next room. Then she came back to me with her eyes sparkling. It took it a moment or two to warm up; by that time the station had gone through one chorus. Just as the voice came in, ours caught up with the other two, so that some girl, who was miles away from there, was singing in three apartments at once, one above the other. Maxine had clasped her hands under her chin and was looking at me across the dishes of food; the words seemed to come out of her eyes. "Here am I—here I'll stay—in your way—until you notice me—" I tried to turn my eyes away; hers followed mine and would not let them go. Her lower lip was quivering. Her eyes grew brighter, brighter, and suddenly were wet and glistening. She didn't say a word; just looked at me, as though she would never get through looking at me. "Here am I—here is love—don't pass us by." Suddenly I couldn't stand it any more. My eyes had tried to escape in every direction, and still she held them within her own. And didn't say a word, a word. "Why do I try—to draw you near me? Why do I sigh—you never hear me—"

And suddenly, without my realizing at just what moment, she spoke. It came to me a second or two later, and what she had said was: "I know you are going to leave me. Something tells me—*you* tell me. The look in your eye—every move you make—tells me."

I didn't answer. Meaning: "Yes, I am going to leave you. Tonight. Right now."

And that cursed infernal thing in there went on. "Don't ever leave me—now that you're here—or I'll have no one to run to." Damn the words, and damn the music, and damn everything connected with that show! It fitted too closely into my own life. I flung myself out of the chair and went in there and snapped it off. But above us and below us it still went on. "Why do I want the thing I cannot hope for? What do I hope for, I wish I knew." And Maxine was still looking at me. An almost invisible silver thread lay beside her nose now, where one tear too many had lost its balance and escaped the watchfulness of her lashes. "Why was I born—to love you?" At last it stopped. The people above us had gone to a movie. The people below us had turned to a prize fight at Forty-Ninth and Eighth Avenue without leaving their chairs.

The coffee in our two cups was stone-cold; the cream she had put in it had gathered around the edges, where it met the cup, in a hollow white ring, leaving the middle black—each cup looked as though it contained a satanic fried egg with a black yolk. This last supper of ours hadn't been a success.

"Oh, I'm so frightened," she said sepulchrally. "What are you going to do, Wade?"

Again I didn't answer.

Again she said, "Won't you speak—and tell me? I'd rather know—and have it over with."

"Why go out of your way to look for trouble?"

"Oh, I know, don't try to tell me," she said all in a breath. "You have something up your sleeve, I get it with every heartbeat!"

"Nothing in particular," I answered facilely. But those were the soothing tactics of last night, of all the nights before, perhaps, but not of tonight. They wouldn't do any more; she had to know. So instantly I belied what I had just said, and told her: "Don't put it that way; not up my *sleeve*. I'm not trying to hide anything from you—I'm going to say good-bye to you tonight."

Bernice's face had expressed fright that afternoon; hers didn't. It looked as though a little death had gathered between her eyes. There was not the insanity of escape, of struggle there; there was the agony of muteness, of somebody gone down in quicksand with only the eyes and forehead showing.

It didn't matter now, I supposed, whether I said anything more. I went on speaking, nevertheless. The drawing room consoling the torture chamber. "I've lost my job. What's the use of going on? Things haven't been any too sweet between us even without that, you know that as well as I do; *now* they'd only be ten times worse. Why drag it out any longer? Don't you think this is the best way?"

"I'll do anything, *anything* under the sun," she said, "anything you want me to, only not to lose you! If it's the job—*I'll* get a job, I'll keep things going for us, Wade! If it's Bernice, if it's that you want to see her as often as you like, why, *see* her, Wade, see her all the time—don't even live with me anymore—I won't say a word, as long as I have you here near me sometimes. Wade, I'll forget there's such a thing as self-respect, I'll forget I'm a *woman* even. What more can I do? Wade, Wade, make it a little easier for me!"

I saw her rise an inch above her chair, as though to come to me, and matter-of-factly motioned her not to. "I don't want you near me, Maxine. My love for you's gotten away from me, there isn't any in me any more."

The pallor of her face literally shone across the table at me; it was awful to see any one suffer like that. I brushed my hand before my eyes to take the sight away. "Don't, oh, *please* don't look at me like that, it goes right through me! I can't stand it. I'm going!"

I made two false moves to rise, and as though she were sending something hypnotic through the air toward me, couldn't seem to get out of the chair at all. Finally I managed to kick it back from me with my heel, stand, and walk out of the room with rigid, forced steps, my head actually turned the other way so as not to see her.

I went into the bedroom, snapped on the light, picked up my valise from beside the wall, looked around me to see if I had left anything out. Meanwhile, not a sound from in there where she was. Not a breath, not a sigh. As though I were alone in the place.

The bureau clock said quarter to eight; it was usually a little slow, though, and until I ride down and everything—

I put out the light, went through the living room, valise in hand, and instead of going back to the kitchen, took the other door, to the little foyer. There I set the grip down a second, not knowing what I was going to call out to her by way of parting, and principally because I wanted to put my hat on properly, and that required two hands.

I had left it over the telephone, always my favorite rack, and as I lifted it off, the phone rang as though the hat had been holding it muffled all along. I chuckled whimsically and picked it up to answer it; it would be too nerve-racking to have to go down the stairs with *that* ringing behind me as though pleading with me to come back, and if I didn't answer it myself, it might bring Maxine out into the foyer, stunned though she seemed to be. I had rather have her stay where she was until after I'd gotten out—I didn't want to have to see that terrible look on her again; I would probably remember it for a long time after this as it was.

"Hello?" I said quietly.

An unmistakable negro drawl greeted me, so exaggerated, in fact, that it almost resembled the accent of a member of some black-face comedy team—Moran and Mack or Amos and Andy. He asked what number I was.

I was so certain there had been a mistake on the line that I told him without further ado, "You've got the wrong party."

"Mistah Wade? You Mistah Wade?" came back engagingly.

"I am. Who're you?"

"All right if I talk to you? Nobody c'n hear?"

"I'm busy. What do you want?"

"Well, look hea', Mistah Wade, this Miss Bernice' do'man— I got a message fo' you."

That was different! "You have?" I cried at once. "What is it?"

"Miss Bernice say for me to tell you she done change her mine—"

I got all cold around the ankles and the wrists.

"—and instead of going to the station from whea' yo' at, will you kinely stop by hea' fo' her and she' go 'long with you."

"Hasn't she left yet?" I cried.

"Nossir, she' busy gettin' ready right *now*."

"Well, then let me talk to her herself a minute, will you?"

"She doan' want to use the outside wire from the 'partment, for *no*body, Mistah Wade, and she hasn't got time to come all the way downstai's hea' and speak over this hea' phoam. She jus' now phoamed down the message to me husself, axin me to tell you."

"All right," I said. "Did she tell you what time she'd be ready?"

"She tole me you could leave any time beginning fum now, and she' be waiting fo' you when you get hea'."

"All right," I repeated a little dissatisfiedly. "Thanks a lot. I'll be there." But as I hung up, I couldn't understand why, when she had been so frightened all along of Tenacity and everybody around her, almost of her very shadow, she would trust a message like that to the doorman instead of speaking to me for a minute herself. But, as he had just said, it might have been the safest way after all.

However, to go there instead of directly to the station, I would have to get a local at Seventy-Second Street, get off a station sooner, walk or taxi several blocks eastward, and then continue on down to Forty-Second Street with her. Which would take considerably more time than the other way. So I knew I'd better leave *then* and not hang around any more if we wanted to make the train—because Bernice might keep me waiting several minutes at *her* place, too.

I picked up the grip, opened the door, glanced back over my shoulder just once, and left—without another word to Maxine. What was there I could have said, anyway? The word "goodbye" wouldn't have comforted her any.

I was down on the street now, walking toward the subway, and the place I had lived in was behind me forever. My farewell to Maxine was to think about her for a few minutes. "Had to leave without a *thing* being arranged between us; if she'd only been modern, instead of 1920! I suppose I should have told her about that compound-interest account in Brooklyn." I went down the steps, dropped my nickel in, sought a bench on the platform, shoved my valise under it, and sat down to wait for the next train. It was already audible in the length of tube between the next station and this, when the turnstile cracked open a second time and Maxine joined me on the platform. She came and sat beside me on the bench. She had no hat, but she had thrown a coat over the housedress she had had on just now in the apartment.

"What do you think you're doing?" I said quietly. "This won't help any; you may as well go on back. I'm not afraid of a row in public, you know; *that* won't stop me, if that's what your game is."

"I didn't come after you to make a scene, Wade," she answered. "I want to ride with you part of the way; five minutes more is better than nothing."

"You're crazy, absolutely out of your mind—" I tried to tell her, but the train came hissing and spitting in and drowned my voice.

She followed me onto the car and sat beside me. People looked at us a little curiously, but I glared at them, and they turned their eyes away. The first few stations drifted by, and she didn't speak. I didn't either, because I had nothing to say; our relationship had ended back *there* as far as I was concerned.

When she did begin to speak at last, it was tragically comic and comically tragic. For she couldn't speak too loud, or the others in the car would hear her (and I could see she didn't want that any more than I did), and yet she must speak loudly enough for me to hear her above the roar of the subway. And I must hear every word, for she hadn't much time—the stations went dropping behind us like beads on a steel-and-electric rosary— and she must win me over, get me to listen, get me to turn back before I got to the end of the line, where Bernice's domain began, where she couldn't follow me any further. I knew that that was what had brought her after me like this—the hope that one supreme, last-minute plea would succeed where all the others had failed. I almost admired her in spite of myself, but, as though the love that was making her go through all this were meant for somebody else altogether and not for me, I was not at all interested. If she knew me as well as she thought she did, why couldn't she see how useless it was? Bernice occupied every cell of my being, there was not a molecule left over for Maxine.

So why even listen to all that she said? I lost most of it in the noise the train was making, anyway. Just once or twice a remark stood out above all the rest, and made me simply wonder at her, simply wonder at her, and fail to understand what I had done to her to make her love me so. Not a trait in me did she neglect to appeal to, did she overlook; the good and the bad, the high and the low. One by one she sounded them out—

"Is Bernice going to give you money, Wade, until you get started again? No? Well, I can give you some, Wade. All you need. I'll give you a whole lot if you'll put off going a while longer—"

Poor little liar, where would she have been able to get it from? But I didn't dare say that aloud, for fear she would think I was intrigued. And I wasn't.

"Would you want Bernice to stop with us a while, so I could get to know her better? I'll gladly ask her out, Wade, if you want me to. Do you think she'd come? I could take a little of the house money and go down to Atlantic City for a little while, and wait until I hear from you—shall I do that, Wade? Shall I do that for you?"

"Don't insult me, Maxine," I murmured close to her face. "That isn't the way—there *isn't* any way! Please go back, kid, won't you? For old times' sake?"

"How far are you going, Wade?"

"Very far."

"How long are you going, Wade?"

"Forever."

There was just one more station to pass now—because I was damned if she was going to get on the local with me at Seventy-Second Street! What was this anyway, a vaudeville show?

"Wade, if I promise to divorce you and let you go, will you stay with me just until we get the divorce?"

"No, not a day longer," I told her simply. "I don't care whether I marry Bernice or not. I'm happy enough just to be with her."

"Do you hate me that much, Wade?" she said.

"I don't hate you at all, Maxine," I answered truthfully. "I like you tonight, like you more than I have the whole past year." I looked at her pityingly and touched her hand for a minute. She sort of shivered. "I like you an awful lot. Don't you think you can find somebody else after a little while, and get me off your mind?"

"But I don't want to," she said innocently.

"Well, will you promise me something?"

"Yes, Wade," she said unqualifiedly.

"I'm going to leave you at the next station; will you promise you won't do anything damn foolish—oh, you know what I mean!"

"I'll promise if you want me to, Wade," she replied surprisingly, "but I wasn't going to, anyway. Because I *know* this isn't forever; one of these days—you *will,* won't you, come back?"

The doors slid open, and I reached for my valise and pulled it out from under my legs. She reached down and helped me with a corner of it that had got wedged in under the seat.

"Good-bye, Max. Try to forgive me, will you?"

"I'm going on down to Forty-Second Street," she explained limply, "because if I get off here, I'll have to pay an extra nickel to cross to the uptown side."

That reminded me, although I was out of the train already. I ran to the window opposite her and pounded on it to attract her attention. Every one else in the car looked around at me, but she had picked up a newspaper some one threw away and was holding it open before her face, as though she were reading it. I guess she was crying behind it, though. The train carried her away. I had wanted to tell her about that compound-interest account over in Brooklyn.

I had just time to light a cigarette and get one drag out of it before my local came in. I had meant to watch from the express window and see just where we passed it, to find out how long I would have to wait, but Maxine had kept my mind occupied. I carried the lighted cigarette in with me anyway—I was so nervous by now I needed it badly—and smoked it secretively out of the little opening between the two cars. Still, it would have been a rotten thing to get arrested *then,* that close to train time.

I got out at the Circle instead of Fiftieth, telling myself it would save time if I walked four blocks *down,* instead of five *up.* Which was undeniable, if you took into consideration the two or three additional minutes it would have taken the train to reach the next station. I walked to her place instead of taking a cab, because it was still early, and because I wanted to see just how nearly ready she was before ordering a taxi and keeping it waiting at the door. It wouldn't take the doorman a minute to do that for us, anyhow, once we had her grips ready at the door.

"I'll leave this with you a minute," I greeted him as I entered, transferring my valise into his kid-gloved and rather reluctant (I noticed) hand.

"Yessir," he said snobbishly, "it's Miss Pascal you want to see, isn't it?" He spoke a purer English than I did myself, evidently had gone to college.

I didn't like his airs, so I answered bellicosely: "You ought to know it is by now; you were the one telephoned me yourself a little while ago to come up here!"

"Nossir, not I," he said urbanely, "you must be mistaken."

This business of contradicting didn't make me like him any better. "I ought to know!" I said. "Are you trying to tell me I'm crazy?" And I gave him a threatening look.

He bore up very well under it; his poise was the last straw— I had taken a decided dislike to him by now. "I didn't say anything about you're being crazy, sir; I said I didn't telephone you, that was all."

"You didn't give me a ring at quarter of eight to the minute and let me know—?" I insisted aggressively.

"Quarter to eight?" he interrupted suavely, with a sort of a Harvard smile transplanted to his iodine-colored face. "Oh, that explains it. I only just went on duty a few minutes before you came in here. It must have been the relief man."

"Is he a colored fellow too?"

"The same as I," he said arrogantly.

"Well, that must be it, then," I remarked lamely, and turned to the elevator.

"Shall I announce you, sir?" he continued. "It's Mr. Wade, isn't it?"

"Yes, it's Wade, if you insist," I sighed weariedly, "but Miss Pascal expects me more than she ever expected any one in her life."

"I see, sir," he remarked ironically, and didn't move toward the switchboard at the back. Evidently, not knowing that we were going away, he had a mistaken impression that this was simply another of our "do-not-disturb" rendezvous.

I got out of the car, the door closed behind me, and I rang her bell. I cocked my head toward the panel and could hear the radio humming away inside. "Eat an apple every day, get to bed by three, take good care of y'self, you belong to me!" She didn't come to let me in; evidently she was in the bedroom putting the finishing touches to her packing and hadn't heard me ring through the noise the Ford was making. So I rang again and drummed lightly on the door with my nails, and rang again, and then again. She must have heard *that;* I had nearly pushed the mother-of-pearl button out of its socket.

But she didn't come to the door. I rang until I was blue in the face, and the ball of my thumb went white with the long-sustained pressure I exerted on it. Still she didn't come to the door. I moved back a pace or two, dug my hands into my pockets, and gazed at the door reproachfully as though it were doing this of its own accord. Then I remembered that I still had her key in my pocket. I had made it the excuse, once, for coming back to see her, but when I had gone away that day I had taken it with me again.

So I fished it out and dug it into the lock, and turned it, and tried the knob, and the door remained more firmly shut than ever. Then I turned it back the other way again, and that opened it. So I saw that it had been open all along, and I had simply locked it myself just now. I could have gone in long ago, instead of standing out there like a fool, but what was she *doing,* anyway, not to have heard me ringing away?

None of the lights were on in the living room, but the dial of the merrymaking radio over in the corner blinked across the dim room at me like a little gold star. And the lights were on in her bedroom and the door had been left ajar. "Bernice," I called in to her, "hurry it up, will you! It isn't early any more!" And I followed this admonition in there personally, pushed the bedroom door out of my way—and stopped. There was no one in there. She wasn't in there.

I crossed the room and looked into the closet—not to see if she was there, but to see how much of her packing she had accomplished. Evidently she had carried it through to completion. Most of the rods were empty, and the few dresses and shoes remaining were lying haphazardly on the floor. Even my untrained eye could tell by that that they had been consigned to the discard. I prodded them idly with my foot and then turned back to the room itself again.

Our glasses were still standing around, the tray she had eaten her lunch from was still there, the striped-brocade chaise longue still flaunted the stain she had made on it when she spilled her drink that time, the very violet satin kimono she had been wearing all afternoon was still lying where I remembered seeing it fall when she threw it off—half over the side of the bed and half on the floor. She was leaving it behind because it had got stained too, I suppose. Only because I had been in the room as often as I had could I tell beyond the shadow of a doubt that everything was completely set for her getaway. Otherwise, it was even less disorderly than I had seen it looking many times before now—on awakening in the mornings for instance. But the fullest perfume bottle of the three was gone from the dressing table, and that photograph she used to have under the mirror looking like a cross between a prizefighter and a Mexican movie star had been torn once across and once up-and-down, and the four resulting pieces neatly piled one on top of the other and dropped into an empty drawer sticking out of its frame like a set of buckteeth. A couple of little touches like this were enough to tell me she was all in readiness to vacate. But then where the hell was she herself?

I knew by now that she was not in the apartment at all, but just to give myself something to do for a second or two, I stuck my head in the two remaining places—serving pantry and bathroom. In one, the gin and vermouth bottles were still side by side on the edge of the vanishing breadboard where I had balanced them when I poured out those last two; in the other, there were just a lot of tiles and dazzling light that was hard on the eyes.

Now it was beginning to trouble me a little; a moment ago it had been just perplexing. I would have phoned down to the doorman and asked him if he had seen her go out, only I knew that he hadn't; he must have thought she was still up here or he wouldn't have been so ready to announce me a while ago. But then he had only come on duty a few minutes before I had got here; the other man would have been the one to ask, and he had gone home now—or wherever doormen went when they were through dooring. But then, anyway, *he* was the very one had telephoned her message to me.

I went back to the bedroom again, lit a cigarette, sat myself worriedly down on the chaise longue, and told myself aloud that I would be a—well, something not very creditable to my mother. A disquieting suspicion settled on me, and then on top of that another that was more than disquieting, that was terrifying, paralyzing. One was that she had gone ahead to the station the way we had originally planned it and was waiting for me *there*—in which case, with me here and she at that end, the train would be gone by the time we located each other. But how was I supposed to know that? Hadn't she *told* me herself to stop by here and call for her! And the worse thought was that she might have gone on to the station and might *not* be waiting there for me—in other words, might have taken an earlier train herself and given me the slip. "But she *wouldn't* do a thing like that to me!" I wailed to myself. I knew, just the same, that if she wanted to badly enough, she could and would. And maybe had. She had had a persecution complex of one sort or another all along, I reminded myself, didn't trust *me* any more than she did any one else; she had told me so to my face not once but several times. The very words rang in my ears: "I met you on the street; how do I know who sent you my way?" What more likely than that she had got leery of me too at the last minute and had made up her mind to play safe and go by herself?

Or else had become conscience-stricken at the eleventh hour at the thought of what she would be doing to Maxine, and decided to leave me behind to her. Or else had just been having a little indoor sport all these weeks, and in the end had gone off with somebody else entirely, letting me hold the bag. This last pleasurable theory was the worst of the lot. It produced a feeling something like taking a red-hot bath with a sunburned back—and scrubbing with a currycomb. But, I told myself, writhing there, what definite proof have you that such couldn't be the case? What do you really know about her private life, after all? She's kept you in the dark from beginning to end—told you never to ask for her on the wire if a man's voice answered, pulled you down emergency staircases with her to keep you from seeing who called on her, cried about something like a child with the colic the night you brought her away from Jerry's party, gone into convulsions of fear because you told another girl that she was corresponding with someone in Detroit. The whole thing smells fishy from beginning to end. Maybe that Marion person had reason to get jealous, at that; maybe there was more truth in it than you know; maybe there *was* something between her and this Sonny Boy individual, and maybe that's where she's gone right now—to Detroit to be with him!

And then a glance at the long, wide vanity table—which was only a couple of feet away from where I was sitting—but a glance *below* it instead of above it as heretofore, sent all my suspicions and torments buzzing away from me like a cloud of mosquitoes when some one has lighted a punk-stick. Three pieces of her baggage were standing there side by side, all latched and strapped and ready to be carried downstairs—a big valise, a much smaller one, and a round, shiny, patent-leather thing, looking like a drum, that was probably a hat- or shoe-box.

I could have jumped up in the air and yelled with surprised relief, felt like kissing the neat little "B.P." marked on each one. I told myself how low I was to have even doubted her for a minute, much less credited her with all kinds of tortuous machinations the way I had. "You have everything going just the way you want it to," I upbraided myself disgustedly, "and instead of being satisfied, you have to go out of your way and look for trouble!" She had probably only just stepped outside for a minute, to get something to eat most likely. Although—I had never known her not to have it sent up from the drugstore downstairs, and tonight in particular, when she claimed she was too busy even to come down and speak to me on the phone, you'd think she would have—oh, well, some other reason then; she would be back in a minute; she had even left the apartment door unlocked.

I shifted to a more relaxed posture on the chaise longue, raised one knee to scratch my calf, put it down again, lighted another cigarette for lack of something better to do—my second since I had come in here. Thought I'd cut down on them once the two of us were settled out there; no sense in lighting one every five minutes the way I did nowa—I had been there longer than that, though; had been there about ten or twelve minutes now, I guessed. I looked over at the clock and—that thing must be wrong! Was that ten past nine, or had it stopped at quarter to two that afternoon and stayed that way? I got up and took a closer look. More than ten past, twelve past—and I had been up there half an hour! If she didn't get back inside of the next five minutes we were just going to make that train by the skin of our teeth—if at all! Until we got the bags downstairs, and by the time we got down to Forty-Second Street through all the traffic! I started pacing back and forth. Wished she'd hurry, what was she doing, wished she'd hurry!

The radio in there was beginning to get on my nerves; it had played nothing but one dance tune after another ever since I had been up there. I liked quieter pieces—and I didn't like music of any kind with my timetables, what was more.

I strode in there to turn it off, put up the room light, which she had left off when she went out, and—there she was!

CHAPTER SEVEN

Gone from me, and just when I thought I had her closest. Turned from something beautiful into something unmentionable, filthy, fit only to be burned or hurriedly smothered with earth and hidden from sight. The mouth that had known how to smile so beautifully remained open now, where death had gone slinking in. The hands that had roamed in my hair were just white things now on the floor. The blue dress (the omen fulfilled!) that had encircled a living body's perfection of form, remained now to cover a carcass.

The icy coating of shock that had coagulated all over me held fast for a moment or two—I even had time to do an unnaturally natural thing: reach out and silence the obscene radio—before it shattered abruptly, and red-hot knives of pain began cutting in at me.

I did things that the sane don't do; got down on my knees, got down on my hands, lay there on my face and gnawed the down of the rug, writhing with the agony that has no seat, knows no physical cause, cannot be stemmed. Tears bubbled from my eyes as though they were percolaters, my nose ran, saliva dripped slowly from between my lips, a drop at a time. My heart pumped under me like a frantic, imprisoned bird caught between me and the floor. I died a hundred times where she had died just once.

The phenomena of grief are banal, after all. Who, seeing some one he loves lie dead, hasn't spoken aloud, hasn't pleaded to her to come back? I did all those things. "Bernice, can't you hear me? It's Wade, your miserable Wade you're doing this to. Open your eyes—just for a *minute*—then you can close them again. Just give me one more look, one more smile, before you go." I drew nearer and nearer to her, like a human being turned alligator. I kissed her at last, and the kiss brought me only horror and recoil. I cried out sharply at the coldness, the goneness of her, and leaped to my feet and drew back quivering. I stared reproachfully over at the thing lying there that had just tricked me like that.

I knew I hadn't kissed *her* just now; *that* was never Bernice. But where *was* she, where had she gone? Oh, more almost than I wanted her back again, I wanted an explanation now, I wanted to be *told.* It was the finality of it that appalled me so, the utter, utter irretrievability. Oh, how much kinder it would have been, how much more consoling, to have belonged to one of those old, gone generations—and been able to kid myself that I would find her again the day I *went* myself. But knowing that the soil, the earth that trees take root in, never, *never* can take wings and rise and speak with a human voice—what was there left for me, what solace had I in the world?

What heaven was there for me, what haven, what hope? *Our* heaven would have been in California, with the things we knew of—the Chevrolet, and she, and I. There would never be any other; we had had our chance, we had muffed it, and—the rest was oblivion.

Exhausted, prostrated—though antipathy to what lay on the floor kept me erect on my feet somehow—drained of almost every feeling but one that hadn't been tapped yet, I stood cowering limply against a wall as though the collar of my coat had caught on a nail and I were suspended there. The knives grew blunted at last, as though the continual driving of them into the same gashes had robbed them of their edge; they gave only a dull ache now. I had no more tears, I had nothing to feed them any more.

In the wake of my ebbing grief came something else—the blind, unreasoning will to preserve myself. I was in a room with that inert mound under the blue dress. The laws of the land said *death* for that. I must get out into the open. I felt as if the walls were likely to close around me and hold me there in a living trap if I stayed a minute longer. The lights shining so brightly in every corner, in every room of this empty silent place seemed much more horrible to me than darkness could possibly have been. I couldn't look at her any more, she seemed to move each time I did. She seemed to cause a spell, a stagnation in the air. Breathe it as deeply as I would, I couldn't get enough of it into my lungs—they seemed to be closing up. It was as though a spark of malevolence had remained behind when all else had fled, and was trying to draw me down, suck me down, into *her* condition.

I turned and beat my way along the wall out into the foyer to the door and flung it open, and the winds of life rushed in again. Fear instantaneously changed its form, and became a fear of the living and not of the dead. I must get *away* from here, *away* from here, and I mustn't let any one see me!

I closed the door behind me and locked it with my key, fingers shaking like ribbons in a breeze. I put the key in my pocket, listened, then crossed the corridor and got the door open that led to the emergency staircase we had used that night. I went down it and down it and down it, not stopping a floor below but all the way to the bottom. On the inside of each heavy door giving out upon a corridor the number of the floor was painted in red. When I had come to the one below "2" I stopped, though the stairs still went further down, and opened it a little and peered out. The soft pinkish lights of the lobby met my eyes, and I heard some people getting out of the elevator to one side of me, without being able to see them because of an angle in the wall.

The ponderous metal slide closed again; evidently the car had just received another call from above. I heard the doorman I had disliked so remark, "Good evening," and mention some one's name. Then a woman's voice said, "Will you get hold of a taxi for us, Leroy?" and I heard the glass doors in front swinging around.

I pushed the staircase door wide and stepped out; there was no one in the lobby. I walked quickly across it to the front door, still spinning idly around, and passed through it into the street.

The doorman was standing out in the middle of the road blowing a little whistle repeatedly and staring fixedly up toward the corner. An elderly lady and a younger one were standing together on the edge of the sidewalk, waiting and looking in the same direction. They had evening wraps on. Neither they nor the doorman turned to look at me as I came out; as a matter of fact he had that very moment turned about to stare in the other direction, toward Fifth, so that his back was now to me altogether.

Though I tried to walk straight, it seemed to me I reeled at every step I took, that those I met would be bound to notice there was something wrong with me. But what more commonplace than an unsteady man making his way along a New York street? I crossed to the other side of Sixth and then turned down it, looking back, always looking crazily back, as though unable to control my neck muscles. An empty cab came along, and thinking I was looking for a taxi, the driver flung the door open for me without even coming to a halt. I took a little run toward it and jumped on, and he cracked the door shut after me, and asked friendlily, "Where to, buddy?"

"Grand Central Station," I shuddered, biting my nails.

I clapped my hand to my breast pocket to make sure I still had the tickets; I could feel the slight stiffness of the pasteboard even through the cloth of my suit—they were there all right. The lights of New York went spinning and hurtling by like shoals of comets, and each time he turned the cab in a new direction, they flattened and elongated themselves against the windows and left tracks and smears of fire across the glass until they had had time to come into focus again. Tall buildings reeled and threatened to topple over on me, or else leaned far back as though we were about to climb up the faces of them, machine and all.

I must get out of this town—the train had left long ago, but there were others—only, I must get out of this town. Where didn't matter; anywhere would do! Montreal, Quebec, some place across the line. And then I thought, shivering, "But they bring you back from those places. Just as quick, even *quicker*. They

expect you to go there, they look for you there." And then I
remembered my grip, standing at that very moment in the lobby
back there. "Oh, I'm gone!" I groaned aloud, and hid my face
behind my sleeves.

I lifted my head again a moment later and looked thoughtfully at the driver's back through foggy, unseeing eyes. What
good would going back for it do, even if I *did* manage to get it
into the cab with me and drive off again without being stopped?
They knew who I was; the very doorman up there knew me by
name, had seen me time and again. The grip wouldn't tell them
anything they didn't know already—

And what good for that matter, I began to tell myself, would
going off like this do? Even if I *did* get out of New York, get to
Quebec, get to Montreal? What was the most I could expect?
To drag out an existence ten times worse than the one Bernice
had foreseen for herself if *she* had quit New York—robbed of
the right to use my own name any longer, cowering at every
shadow that crossed my path, fleeing abruptly and silently
from one place to the next as though pursued by ghosts or pos-
sessed of devils. Ah, no! To face such a future, to plunge into
it, was not cowardice—was the utmost bravery, required more
courage than I had. I hadn't the guts, the lust for life anymore
that *that* took. After all, what was there so sweet about life any
longer to make it worth fighting for at such a price? What happiness was there left for me in this world even if I stood
acquitted of all suspicion at that very moment? Gray days and
endless nights without *her.* Month after month of them, year
after year of them.

Oh, I had no one to stand at my shoulder and say in my ear,
"A year from now, six months from now, it will still hurt perhaps when you remember her, but you won't remember her con-
stantly all day long or all through the night; days will have color
and nights will have dawns. And a year is such a small part of
a lifetime—take a sporting chance and stick it out!" And if I *had*
had, I wouldn't have believed them anyway, would have thrown
the lie in their teeth. I was so sure that all my life from now on

was going to be like tonight. So I made up my mind and I lifted my hand and I knocked on the glass.

"Never mind about the station," I said. "Take me back to 55th Street again."

And I wasn't going back for my grip, I was going back to get what was waiting for me. And if nothing was waiting for me yet, why I was going to look it up myself. *I* was the coward, not the brave guy—I didn't have the stuff in me, the starch, the *sand,* to face all those hours and weeks and months feeling the way I did: heartbroken, weary, alone, and bereft. This way was much quicker and easier.

When we got back to the door, I simply left him without a word and walked into the lobby. I already felt much calmer than I had at any time since earlier in the day. I even felt calmer than when I still thought she and I were going to make our getaway together. I had been all worked up with anticipation then. This was a soothing lassitude, on the contrary, that almost made me want to drop down in the first comfortable chair that came along and wait for things to turn up.

The doorman looked at me in surprise; evidently he had still thought I was upstairs all this time. "Why, *I* didn't see you come down in the ele—!" he started to say to me.

"Phone for the police," I interrupted laconically, stepping into the car. "Send them up to Miss Pascal's apartment. I'll be up there." And I motioned the openmouthed operator to go ahead.

"Anything wrong, sir?" he finally managed to articulate.

"What's that of *your* business?" I told him placidly.

He kept the car standing there with the door open after he had let me off, dying to get a look in after I opened the door, I suppose. "Go on down, will you!" I snarled. "What are you standing there for? There's nothing to see."

With which he reluctantly cut himself off from me behind the panel and was gone.

I unlocked the door and went in once more, leaving it wide open so that that creepy feeling of being alone in there wouldn't come back. I turned a chair around so that it faced away from her, sat down in it, lit a cigarette, and directed my gaze out through the open door upon the elevator door opposite, which was in a direct line from where I was sitting. Something kept trying to pull my head around in the other direction; I had to stiffen the muscles of my neck to resist it. I kept praying I could hold out until they came, and not give in and look. "Bernice," I murmured, "what more do you want of me? Let me be."

When I was in the act of lighting a fresh cigarette from the stump of the old, they finally got there. They came filing across the corridor directly toward me, getting bigger and bigger all the time as they got nearer, while the chair and I seemed to grow smaller and smaller. As they entered the living room from the foyer, all I could see any more were their huge feet and the mammoth legs of their trousers. If they didn't stop soon, they'd go over me, and I'd be crushed under their gigantic soles—my head sort of rolled over on my shoulder, and then I pulled it back again and everything was the right size once more.

"She dead?" one of them said to me, taking his eyes off the floor.

"Long time now," I answered.

"You do it?" the same one said. He seemed to be asking the questions to satisfy his own personal curiosity, just as one man will go up to another on a street corner where a crowd has collected and ask what the trouble is. Others were busying themselves with her, I could tell without turning around; he seemed to have nothing to do for a minute, hence his interrogation of me.

"There she is," I said listlessly, "and here I am. What more do you want?"

"Plenty," he said, "you're talking to an officer, and don't forget it!" And he sent his fist hurtling into the side of my face. There was a flash of fire before my eyes, and I went over on the floor, chair and all. The pain was gone an instant after the blow, and it felt so *lazy*, so effortless, lying there prone like that, that I wanted to let my eyes close and not lift a finger toward getting up again. But the thought that *she* was on the floor too, some-where just a little in back of me, made me come to and pick myself up again. I left the chair where it was.

"Pick it up," he ordered truculently, "and next time don't get so wise!"

I set it on its feet again and looked at him inquiringly.

"Siddown," he thundered. "We're *comin'* to you!"

But it seemed to take them hours to do so. People kept com-ing in and coming in, some in uniform and some without, some in white coats, some carrying satchels—all their attention was focused on *her.* Once or twice I dared to turn and look, because there were so many of them around her that I couldn't see her any more—bending over her, squatting down on their haunches, pawing her, doing things that I couldn't understand. A man car-rying a tripod came in at one time and set it up just inside the door, and they all drew back from her, out of the way, and there was a flash of diamond-white light and a puff of smoke. Then he went even nearer her, almost stood directly above her, and there was another flash and another puff. Then he picked up the tripod and went out. I remember thinking vaguely that he must be a reporter, but it seems not, because later another man with a tripod came out of the emergency-staircase door, and the moment they saw him, two of them rushed out and came to blows with him. They broke the tripod, flung him into the ele-vator, and he was taken downstairs.

About midnight or one in the morning, they took me into Bernice's bedroom and shut the door. The ones in uniform seemed to be playing a minor part by this time. There was one of them standing just inside the door with his hands clasped behind him, but all the others in the room were with-out uniforms. One of them had turned Bernice's vanity table into a desk and was sitting beside it writing on a thick sten-ographic pad. The three pieces of baggage were gone from un-derneath it.

"Siddown!" I was told.

I sat down and leaned forward over my knees.

When they were through looking at me—and only because I was past caring about anything any more was I able to bear the awful, baleful scrutiny from all sides—they began to ask me questions. Or rather one in particular did. Sometimes, during all this, he'd get up as though he were through, and I'd think he had left the room, only to have him suddenly ask me something over my shoulder.

"Your name's Wade," they told me. "How old are you?"

"Twenty-six."

"How long have you known her?"

"About a month, I guess."

"What'd you do it for?"

"I don't know."

Two or three of them advanced on me threateningly. "What'd you do it for?" he roared a second time.

"Because I loved her."

The blow I got this time was from the back; I stumbled forward out of the chair, went down on both hands and struck my head against the edge of the thick glass slab that covered the vanity table. It opened the skin a little above one eye.

"Get up; you're not hurt," he informed me. "Now, are you gonna answer or aren't you! Wait a minute," he interrupted himself, "lemme ask you something else; where were you going with her tonight?"

"California." I reached in my pocket, took out the tickets, and passed them to him.

When he was through looking at them he said, "Why were you going out there?"

"To live," I said simply.

He got up and went away; I kept looking at the place he had just been sitting in. Suddenly he whipped out from somewhere in back of me, "Well, if she was going with you, what'd you do it for?"

"'Cause she backed out at the last minute," I said instantly, without turning around.

"Now we're gettin' some place," he remarked to the others, and came around in front of me and sat down again.

Most of the questions after that were easy to answer; all I had to keep remembering was that I had done it because she had changed her mind at the very last and refused to go with me—everything followed from that quite naturally. Toward the end, possibly because I was answering just as they seemed to want me to, they even became less threatening, dropped their voices a pitch or two.

Then at the very last, when it all seemed clear sailing, everything went wrong again. He had just told me that they were going to draw up a confession then and there and have me sign it, and had already ordered the policeman to take me into the other room and hold me there until it was ready—when he motioned me back again to where I had been sitting and said, "Suppose you run through it in your own words; take this down, George, and don't miss anything." Then to me again, "All right—you came up here a little after nine, and you found her all packed and ready for you. And then she said she wasn't going. Now go on from there."

I was so tired already; I couldn't understand what more they wanted! I'd already said I'd done it; over and over I'd said I'd done it. I'd always thought they only questioned you like this when you denied a thing, not when you admitted it. I swallowed to moisten my throat, and said: "She said she wasn't going. She said I didn't have enough money. I begged her and she wouldn't listen to me—" And right while I was speaking, I kept thinking, "Where am I going to say I got the gun? What am I going to say I did with it afterward?" So far, I noticed, they hadn't asked me a word about that. "So then I told her I was going alone. She said, all right, go ahead. So I went downstairs by the emergency staircase; my bag was in the lobby and the doorman was outside in front of the house. He didn't see me. I opened the bag and took the gun out. I went running all the way up the stairs again. I had her key, and I opened the door and went in again. I asked her for the last time if she would come with me, and she said no, so I shot her. I threw the gun out of the window right after I'd done it—"

I noticed that they'd all grown very quiet and were staring at me curiously; I saw one or two of them exchange looks with one another.

"How many bullets did you give her?" the man before me asked brutally.

Why hadn't I thought of that? Why hadn't I taken a look the whole time I was alone with her, and noticed?

"I don't remember," I said. "I think I fired two or three times—"

The man before me turned around and said, "You got that, George?"

"That's no good," someone else expostulated. "Why don't you find out what he's up to!"

"You lemme do this my own way, Dowlan!" he bellowed back, and glared at him to silence him. "I know what I'm doing!" I heard the door open and shut behind me, and he looked up, over and beyond me, and said, "You bring it with you? Good! Give it to George here." And a typewriter of the portable variety was brought forward and placed on the vanity table. After which they ordered the policeman to take me outside to the other room, "until we tell you to bring him back again."

No sooner had the door closed after me than I heard the keys of the typewriter begin to click at breakneck speed. The apartment door still stood wide open, but there was a policeman standing before it, and another one opposite him mounting guard over the elevator door. In the living room itself, a man was going around examining the knobs on the doors and other odds and ends, but evidently not in a professional capacity, for he had no magnifying glass. Yet when he turned my way, I saw that he had some sort of a little thing screwed into his eye. Another was sitting before a drawer that had been removed bodily from some article of furniture and going painstakingly through a cloud of papers it contained. Most of them looked like bills from a distance. *She* was gone now; she had evidently been taken away while I was inside. It made things a little more bearable for me.

I asked the policeman to let me go to the bathroom, and the answer I got was more unpleasant than amusing. I sat down in the chair I had occupied originally.

The typewriter stopped after awhile, and you could hear their voices in the other room, but not what they were saying. I started to light a cigarette, and the policeman snarled, "Who told you to go ahead and smoke?"

The man who had been looking at the doorknobs and things lifted his head and said, "Let him smoke, Sheehan. He hasn't long to do it in."

"And it won't be smoker's heart that'll stop him, either," the policeman agreed.

The typewriter recommenced all at once, as though some point that had momentarily clogged its progress had just been settled. Then, a little while after that, a bulb in one of the lamps burnt out, from overuse no doubt, and went dark.

"She had a nice place here," the policeman remarked thoughtfully.

"Did you ever know one that didn't?" the man going over the bills snapped.

I noticed for the first time that the other one, the doorknob fellow, was no longer there, had gone without my even realizing it. But I was so tired; everything was bathed in a mist!

The typewriter stopped again. Then almost at once, this second time, the bedroom door opened, and they motioned to the policeman with their heads.

He brought me in again. "Lock the door," the one who had asked me most of the questions the time before ordered. The room was already full of smoke; Bernice's familiar things looked funny through it. Between that and the state my eyes were in, I could hardly see their faces straight anymore.

"Read him what you got there, George," I heard him say. "His own words. From where she told him she wasn't going with him."

The man who had been using the vanity table for a desk all along began to read some typed sheets aloud. "—so I shot her. I threw the gun out of the window right after I'd done it—"

When he was through, the other one gave me a crafty sort of a smile and said, with remarkable (for him) moderation, "You admit you done it in just that way, do you? And you're ready to sign what he just read to you, are you?"

"Yes," I said dully.

Someone else said something to him under his breath that I didn't quite catch, whereupon he whirled around fiercely and burst out: "Tell that to your grandmother! He's as sane as I am! He's yellow, that's what's the matter with him!"

Then turning back to me, again with unwonted restraint, he continued, "Suppose we were to make a few changes in that—just a coupla things here and there—suppose you were too excited to remember everything just the way it happened, and we were to sort of, now, help it along for you—would you still sign it?"

"I told you I did it," I murmured, "and I'll sign anything you want me to, any way you put it."

He seemed almost more surprised than gratified for a moment, but he didn't waste any time. The man at the desk handed him several typed sheets; whether they were the same ones he had read or not I couldn't tell. He patted them into shape and put them down beside him without looking at them, took a fountain pen out of his pocket and held it toward me, saying: "All right, then sign *this!* This is the way it really happened."

I took the pen from him, wrote my name where he showed me to on the paper he handed me, and then passed both back to him—or rather the pen alone, for he had never taken his hand from the paper for an instant.

"That's that!" he said, folding the papers and inserting them into the inside pocket of his coat with an air of ponderous satisfaction. "You didn't shoot her; you strangled her to death with your hands, like we found her!" And giving those around him the wink, he added, "Now bring on your lawyers!"

They asked me a few desultory questions after that, but more in the manner of horseplay than a serious attempt to find out anything further. Such as: Had I really forgotten I had choked her and imagined I had shot her, or had I deliberately invented the story about running down the staircase and getting a gun out of my grip? And if so, why?

"I don't know why," I said in a half-audible voice. "Maybe because I'm romantic. Maybe because it's the first time I ever did a thing like this, and I wanted to make it sound better than it really was." And to myself I added, "Or maybe because I didn't do it at all in the first place."

I no longer knew whether I had or hadn't; I was no longer sure. I had been telling them I had for so long that it seemed to me I must have after all. I found myself actually forgetting that I hadn't seen her at all from the moment I left her at five in the afternoon to get the tickets until the time I found her lying on the floor—found myself actually beginning to believe that I *had* found her still alive, *had* spoken to her when I came back at nine. It was literally with surprise that I at last stopped short and reminded myself, "But she was already *gone* when you got back; somebody else *must* have done it!"

Oh, I no longer knew whether I was sane or insane, awake or dreaming; no longer cared! All I knew was, every breath I drew was hellfire, every minute that passed was a crucifixion.

It was growing lighter outside the windows now, like so many times when I had been up in this room with her. I knew just where the first splashes of pearl and pink were going to hit against the wall; knew just at what point they would begin to spread like blisters and reach upward toward the ceiling and downward toward the floor. But just before it all began, they clicked a steel ring over my wrist and at last made ready to depart.

As they brought me out of the bedroom into the living room, I turned and asked if I couldn't go to the bathroom. So the one whose wrist was joined to mine unwillingly turned aside and stood at my shoulder for a minute. After that they took me out to the elevator—Bernice's apartment vanished forever behind the vertical metal trap—and I stood in the exact middle of all of them, like someone popular, like someone surrounded by all his friends, as we went down to the street.

Even at that unearthly hour, a handful of ghouls had gathered around the street door, or maybe they had been standing there all night like that, I don't know—and there was another one of those starlike flashes and puffs of smoke, because it was still dim out on the street. But this time the men with me didn't attempt to break the camera or drive the perpetrator away. Then, just as they were putting me in a car at the curb, another diversion occurred; I heard a protesting, argumentative voice somewhere in back of me. "I been waitin' all night," it said, "they wouldn't even lemme go in the lobby! He owes me twenty-four dollars, and six more for overtime—" I heard them all laughing, and I turned and saw a man standing there, pale in the face and sweating with anxiety. "He rode all the way down to Gran' Central with me—" he said. Meanwhile there was another one of those skyrocket flashes, followed by a tart smell, so close to me this time that I jumped and collided against the man I was manacled to. But by its light I recognized the protesting individual as the cabdriver I had hired at one time or another last night and then left standing before the door—just when, I wasn't sure, or why, or whether I really *hadn't* paid him as he said.

The man with me flicked me on the arm and said humorously, "Y'got any money on you?"

"Tell him to get a cop and have me pinched," I answered stonily, and the irony of saying such a thing at such a time only dawned on me after I'd heard the roar of appreciation that went up on all sides. I didn't smile.

They ushered me in the car and sat on each side of me, and we drove off down the streets of New York in the beginning of the morning light, with batches of lights going out everywhere, like that single bulb in Bernice's living room had gone out a while back. But what was dawn and the start of the day for every one else was dusk and the ending of it for me.

But if it *was* dusk, and it *was* the end of my day, it seemed to go on forever and forever; the night that I prayed and yearned incessantly for seemed never to begin. Sometimes I used to wonder if what I had mistaken for an indictment hadn't really been my trial after all, and I had been sentenced to life imprisonment without realizing it. I used to go into a cold sweat whenever it occurred to me that I *might* get life or twenty years instead of what I wanted. "Gee, it's *got* to be that!" I moaned, walking back and forth. "It's little enough to ask for! Those that *don't* want it always get it—why shouldn't I?"

Maxine came to see me—it seemed long afterward, but it may have only been a few days; all I know is, they brought me out one time, and she was on the other side of a wire screen. And she looked so bad, so old, so forlorn—it almost seemed I must be visiting her, and not she me.

"Why did you leave me that night?" she said tenderly. "This wouldn't have happened to you—"

"How is it out today?" I said. "Very warm, or is it cooler than it was before?"

She saw what I meant, so she answered, "It's pretty warm, warmer than it was yesterday—"

"Where do you live now, Maxine?" I said. "In the same place?"

"Oh, no," she said. "I've been in the hospital; I just got out yesterday, that's why I couldn't come to you any sooner."

"Feeling all right now?" I asked, letting my eyes stray around vacantly.

"Yes," she said readily, "it was just the suddenness of the thing, on top of everything else—" Then she went on, "I have a lawyer for you; he'll help you out of this."

"I don't want a lawyer," I said.

"I want you to tell him *everything,* when he comes to see you," she pleaded vibrantly. "He's the best I could get hold of; it's not too late yet—that awful confession, what did they do, grill it out of you?—there's still every chance in the world, if you—"

"All I want," I told her, "is to get it over with."

"Wade, for *my* sake, if not your own," she begged. "Won't you give me this one last break? It's taken every cent I had—"

"No, Maxine, no! I *want* to go!"

"Wade, darling," she groaned, "for Bernice's sake, then. She wouldn't want you, she wouldn't want any one to have this happen—she was too nice a girl!"

"Bernice is gone," I answered. "There isn't any more Bernice."

"Wade, you *didn't* do it, you *know* you didn't! You're lying your very life away!"

"I *did* it, Maxine!" I shouted passionately at her at last. "I choked her to death with my own hands! *Now* will you believe me? *Now* will you go away and leave me alone?"

"God forgive you for what you're doing to the two of us!" was the last thing she said.

The lawyer's name was Berenson. He came to see me the next day, and scowl as I would that I didn't want to see any one, wouldn't leave my cell I was brought in to him. It wasn't important enough one way or the other, after all, for me to dig my heels between the boards of the floor and put up a physical struggle about.

"Your poor wife," one of the first things he said to me was, "sold the very wedding ring off her finger, sold her radio, sold everything, to be able to get someone's services in your defense. At that, the money she came to me with, wouldn't have paid for the first half-hour's conference we had. I have it put aside in my safe right now, and she's welcome to it back the day the trial ends—no matter what the outcome. Now believe that or not, Wade, whichever you prefer!"

"I'd believe anything these days," I told him.

"I've taken this case over," he said, "because I'm *interested* in it—because I have a hunch it's going to turn out to be the biggest case in years—and because I think I can squeeze enough prestige out of it before I'm through to last me the rest of my career. Do you get me?"

"No," I said, "I don't. Y'better lay off it, if it's prestige you're after, because you've got a client that doesn't *want* to be defended and a case that *can't* be won!"

"Why can't it?" he snapped. "You didn't kill her!"

"Didn't I? *I* say I did," I said sullenly. "How do *you* know I didn't?"

"You were all the way down at Grand Central in a cab the first time," he said, "and you turned around and went back there. If *you'd* done it, nothing could have gotten you within a mile of that place that night!"

"Why not?" I decided. "I couldn't get away with it, that was all."

"You would have gone to the nearest police station, then—not to the very room she was lying in, *alone.* Don't try to tell me; I ought to know a little about human nature by now!"

"All right, Mr. Berenson," I said, "build up your beautiful case! Build it sky-high! And when you've got it all spic and span and foolproof, I'm going to stand up there in the stand just the same and tell the world I killed Bernice Pascal!"

"You think you're the kingpin in this, don't you, Wade!" he told me scathingly. "You think the whole case is centered around *you* and whether you're guilty or whether you're not! Well, let me *tell* you, my dear boy, you're not as important in this affair as that very colored girl she had working for her—you're nothing more than the sucker that's taking the rap!" He opened a dull silver cigarette case and held it toward me with the contemptuous air of some one feeding peanuts to a rather smelly animal in the zoo. "You loved her, didn't you?" he said.

In thinking it over after he'd gone, I realized that it was at about this point I began to fall for him.

"Maybe I didn't!" I assented wistfully.

"Your wife told me as much," he went on. "She had an idea that that might be the reason for your whole fool attitude from the time of the arrest. Pascal's gone, so you don't give a damn one way or the other now."

"Which is just about the size of it," I said stiffly, "and my own privilege in the bargain."

"Fair enough," he agreed, "but it makes a pretty poor showing, when you come right down to it. Leaving yourself out of it altogether, you're letting the *real* guys that killed the woman you love get away with murder. You don't seem to feel that you *owe* that much to her—to get busy and settle accounts for her. In other words, Wade, you may be standing up and telling the world that you killed her—but what you're telling yourself, and *her,* is that she's not worth avenging! That she deserves what she got!"

"God knows that isn't true!" I burst out. "I'd choke the rats that did it with my own hands if I only knew who they—"

Then I knew by the smile on his face that I had told him I hadn't done it.

"I'm taking the case, Wade," he let me know. "I mayn't be able to keep you out of the chair, but at least I'll keep you out of the witness box!"

But I went back to the cell shaking my head and thinking, "What good is it if he *does* get the right guys? What good is it if I *do* get even for her? What good is *any*thing? Will it bring *her* back?"

I must have been a funny client, though! After that first day, I told Berenson anything he wanted to know, didn't hold back a thing—and yet never again, after that first slip of the tongue, would I admit I *hadn't* done it. I noticed he didn't waste much time arguing out that point with me (and to me it seemed all that mattered in the whole thing: whether I said I *did* do it or said I *didn't* do it) but seemed more interested in a whole lot of other things, side issues like the party at Jerry's that Saturday night, and the way Bernice had once begged me to stop seeing her, and the man that had answered her phone the night I had called her from the restaurant, and the way I had met Marion on the street and she had had a spasm of jealousy over what I told her, and so on.

Sometimes I would tell him things that it seemed to me he should have gone into ecstasies over, should have congratulated me on remembering, and he would brush them impatiently aside and remark, "That's not a bit of good to me." And then again, he would suddenly flap his wings and lose feathers all over the room about some trivial detail that didn't have the utmost bearing on the case, as far as I could see. I used to wonder sometimes if he was really a good lawyer.

For instance, during one of our talks I suddenly recalled how I had walked out of Bernice's place the first night I met her, wearing somebody else's hat by mistake. Not only that, but by some quirk of memory the size and make of it even came back to me! I at once gave him the dope on it, afraid I might forget all about it again. "Y'better put that down," I advised, "size 6 ⅜! And inside the hatband it said *Boulevard des Capucines!*" And waited for him to fall all over me when he heard it. My life was pretty colorless, I guess.

All he said was, "Don't let's waste time, Wade; I'm not running the fashion column for men in the theater programs." And then, on the other hand, one time when I was trying to recall, more for my own morbid satisfaction than his benefit, what my last words to her had been when I left there the afternoon it happened, I recollected that they hadn't been to her at all, but to Tenacity, who had stopped me on my way out to ask me if Bernice was "fixing to fire her, or what?" He no sooner heard that than he stopped me then and there and demanded excitedly, "Why didn't you tell me that before? That the colored girl was still in the place when you left! I've had a feeling all along that she'd be our trump card in this!"

I didn't follow him, and gave him a look that told him so.

"I'd like to bet," he said, slapping his knee, "that she was drawing pay from other sources besides the wages Pascal paid her!"

I *still* didn't get him but no longer bothered signaling the fact. "I read in one of the tabs," I said, "that they had her down at headquarters the day after, questioning her. I think they're going to use her as a witness against me—"

"Let me get my hands on her!" he said viciously. "*I'll* find out who Pascal's friends were!"

"Anyway, she left the place herself five minutes after I did that afternoon," I remarked indifferently. "The doorman and the elevator man both backed her up on that, according to what the paper—"

"Oh, her alibi's as good as gold," he interrupted caustically. "A little too good, if you want to know the way I feel about it. She wasn't satisfied with asking the doorman what time it was—she had to let her Ingersoll slip out of her hand while she was pretending to wind it and break the crystal on the floor, and then make some remark about that meaning bad luck, a death in the house or something to that effect. And the doorman, being colored himself, wasn't likely to forget that when the time came. Then on *top* of that, as though that weren't enough, she conveniently remembered some phone message Pascal had asked her to deliver, and used the downstairs phone—as though she couldn't have thought of that while she was still upstairs!"

"Oh, that must've been to *me,*" I said reflectively and then again, "No, that's right, it was a man, and it didn't come until quarter to—"

"It wasn't to you at all," he said sourly. "I got the whole story. It was to some girlfriend of Pascal's, and the call never went through because she'd been dispossessed for having too many brawls in her place. This clever colored wench has to throw a fit of giggling when she hears that, pretending it struck her so funny, and repeat the whole thing to the doorman word for word. Take it from me, she knew what was coming and wanted to *impress* every one with the fact that she was going home at quarter to five. I'd like to bet that other days no one even saw her come and go!"

I remembered something then and told him: "Wait a minute, you've got the whole thing wrong. *That* wasn't the time she made that call—she'd already made it upstairs right in front of me and Bernice. Bernice called her in the room specially for that, and I remember she said she didn't have to look the number up; she knew it by heart. And *that* was when they told her they were dispossessed—not down in the lobby at all."

"Well, it's damn queer, then," he said, "that it should strike her so funny fifteen floors below that she has to break out laughing all over the place until the doorman himself told her not to make so much noise; she'd get him in trouble. I never yet heard of any colored Englishwomen, did you?"

"Maybe she's from the British West Indies," I suggested unwittingly.

He gave me an indescribable look and shook his head to himself. "*You* never killed Bernice Pascal," he said in a low voice. I turned my face aside with sharp impatience. "No, it's ten to one that what she did downstairs, the coon I mean," he went on, "was step over to the phone and send out the tip-off that Pascal was packing and getting ready to skip out of New York that night. And then went over to the doorman and pretended that the call she had just made was the first one, the one you *heard* her make upstairs. Just let her take the stand—*I'll* get it out of her. They'll wish they had paid her fare to California, whoever they are!"

I was so little interested, however, in what his plans were, and in fact in the whole trial itself, that I didn't even know what date had been set for it. I'd only glanced at a paper on two occasions since they'd brought me here, and as it nearly turned my stomach to see Bernice's face splashed all over the pages in gummy ink—with words like "Butterfly" and "Slain Beauty" and "Queen of Hearts" written above it—and encounter column after column of a diary that I knew damn well she'd never written, I didn't repeat the attempt. It was tough enough to have lost her without having to share her with the entire world.

And Berenson, either because he had so much else on his mind that it never occurred to him or because he took it for granted that I already knew, never said a word to me about it either. So the first I knew about when it was due to begin was the morning of the very day itself, when the turnkey suggested to me not unkindly that I "oughta take a shave for myself."

"Why?" I said, "the cement walls aren't complaining, are they?"

"They'll be taking pictures of you today in court," he said, "and you look like hell. You wanta make a good impression on the jury, don't ya?"

"Oh, is it *today?*" I said, and I went ahead and "took a shave for myself." And I mean just that, for *myself,* and not for the jury or anybody else.

And so it began—and all I did after that was *sit* there, day after day, and day after day. I couldn't even understand what they were talking about most of the time. They'd bring me in each morning and sit me down—and I always sat in the same place—and then at noon they'd take me back again, and then early in the afternoon they'd bring me in again, and then *late* in the afternoon they'd take me out again. And the next day the whole dreary thing would start over again. All I did was go in and out of that room and *sit* there—with every one in the back of the room staring their eyes out at me.

At the end of the first week, when I was confident the thing must be nearly over, I found out through Berenson that they'd only just gotten through picking out jurors. When he saw the look on my face, he said, "Wade, this *is* an interesting case; most men in your shoes would hug every delay!"

He told me Maxine had been present every day. "Tell her to go on home!" I said harshly. "Hasn't she got enough decency to stay away from here?"

The second week it became a little more comprehensible; at least they stopped asking jurors what business they were in and whether they were opposed to capital punishment, and began to have a succession of people on the stand—who spoke of things more closely related to me. But presently I had heard the banal, monotonous story so often, from so many different angles, that I could have yelled my lungs out for mercy. In sheer self-defense I fell into the habit of staring hypnotically out of the nearest of the wide, tall windows. The sun came pouring in through them almost without exception during the whole of this time, and if I watched attentively enough, I could see little grains of dust floating around in it and making patterns. But at the end of one session Berenson took occasion to warn me against doing that. He said it made me seem callous, hard-boiled, would make a bad impression on the jury. "Oh, jury be damned!" I thought to myself wearily.

Among those called on as witnesses was Leroy, Bernice's Harvard-accent doorman. His last name was Devereaux, I found out. He came to court without his uniform and wearing a fuzzy caramel-colored suit with patch pockets and a half belt in back that would have driven any college freshman insane with longing. With this went beige spats, four inches of brown-silk handkerchief hanging out of his breast pocket, and, I am almost positive, a walking stick hanging up somewhere in the courthouse checkroom.

He sat up there at elegant ease, and no man in the room could match his English. It was really as delightful as it was instructive to listen to him speak, but I noticed the judge had to turn his head away several times during the course of the cross-questioning.

Leroy told how I had appeared about nine in Bernice's lobby, passed a grip I was carrying to him, and then insisted I had just had a message from him on her behalf to come up there, which he again flatly denied having sent me, just as he had that night. This point held them up for fully half an hour, and only the liquidity of Leroy's vowels kept me from returning to look out of the window again in spite of Berenson's admonition. When they had finally decided that it was the relief man who had sent the message (and I saw Berenson give me a triumphant look, but what about I couldn't imagine), Leroy was allowed to go ahead. He told them he had asked me if I wanted to be announced, whereupon (the "whereupon" was his own, too) I had given him an odd look and remarked: "Miss Pascal expects *me* more than she ever expected any one in her life." At which point I heard a buzz of excitement rise from the onlookers at the back of the room. The judge struck the desk with his mallet, and when they had grown quiet again, Westman, the prosecuting attorney, asked Leroy to describe the look he said I had given him.

"It was a, I should say a *sinister* look," Leroy said.

I had never known just how to pronounce that word until I heard him use it.

"Explain what you mean," Westman said.

"It was the look of a man who is dangerous, who is capable of almost anything. Well, there's no other word for it, it was a sinister look, that was all," Leroy informed him dogmatically.

I felt like jumping up then and there and protesting that it couldn't have been that kind of a look because I hadn't known how to pronounce the word at the time.

"Has the defendant that look on him now?" Westman went on.

Leroy turned to look at me, and I certainly *had,* even if I'd never had it before; I was glaring at him with all my might. "Thoroughly," he said, turning away again in a hurry.

From there he went on to say that he had next seen me at about quarter to ten, and had been very much taken aback, because I was going *in* again like the time before, and he hadn't seen me come out at all. And that I had told him to get the police, I would be up in Bernice's apartment.

When Berenson took him over, he asked him a few desultory questions first, and then suddenly skipped all the intermediate evidence to inquire with beguiling deference what his, Leroy's, theory was as to how I had managed to leave the building without being seen either by himself or the elevator operator. I couldn't figure out why he was asking that at *this* late day. The whole town, or anyway as large a part of it as was following the case, knew by this time I had come down the emergency staircase when neither of them were looking. That had been in the confession I had signed.

Leroy smiled tolerantly and said, "We all know how he accomplished that—" and repeated what I had done.

"In that case," Berenson said quickly, "would it have been equally possible for any one else to have used the same staircase that evening—and *not* be seen by you or any one in the lobby?"

"I don't see why not," Leroy replied haughtily. "I'm kept quite busy before the house procuring cars. Especially around dinnertime. And after all, I don't expect people to slink—"

"Answer yes or no!" Berenson snapped. "Would it have been equally possible for any one else to have come down those stairs that night and left the building without being seen by you?"

"Yes," Leroy answered sulkily. I suppose he didn't like to be confined to one-syllable words because there wasn't as much opportunity to pronounce them beautifully.

"That's all," Berenson said. Leroy uncoiled himself, stood up so that every one would have a fair chance to admire and profit by his attire, and left the stand walking on air. Some rude damsel in back tittered.

Berenson called someone I'd never seen before in his place. Also colored. I began to wonder if Bernice and I were the only white people involved in this case. This one, it soon turned out, was the reliefman. He had been on duty, he said, from seven until nine that evening. He had *not* telephoned any message to me from Bernice. He had not telephoned any message to anybody from Bernice. He had not telephoned any message to anybody from *anybody.* Every dwelling in the building had its own private phone; the only calls he had received were incoming ones, there had only been two of those, and one had been a wrong number and the other a lady who wished to have her husband informed, when he got home, that he was to come right out again and meet her at Tony's, *Jimmy* was there. "*Your* witness," Berenson said after a sufficient amount of this.

I now understood his triumphant look to me awhile back, when Leroy had been on the stand, and the phone message I had gotten had been credited to the relief man. But I still didn't understand what he had to be, feel, or look triumphant about. After all, even if the message was proven to be fake (and I was beginning to think it was myself, because the relief man's voice didn't even approach the Octavus-Roy-Cohen dialect that had greeted my ears over the wire), that didn't prove that I hadn't gone up there and done it myself anyway. It merely suggested feebly, if one were inclined to be prejudiced in my favor, that I had been framed by some person or persons unknown. And on the other hand, there was only my word for it that there *had* been any such message at all. Only Maxine and I had been there when the phone rang; what chance had Berenson of proving it to the jury?

I noticed that Westman himself considered this point so immaterial to the evidence that he didn't even try very hard to shake the relief man's insistence on not having sent the call, just let him go after a question or two. When the case was adjourned for that day, Berenson came up to me almost exuberantly, he seemed so pleased with the way things had gone, and giving my biceps a furtive, encouraging grip, breathed, "Wait'll to-morrow, kid! It's going to start getting rosy from now on. They're calling Tenacity!"

I had a peculiar dream that night in the cell of a sort of black Bernice, whom I was very much in love with, but the color of whose skin kept rubbing off on my clothes every time I went near her. And each time it did, she sort of cried out in pain, so that my heart was wrung.

Next day, about halfway through the morning's session, the famous Tenacity's name was at last called. "Tenacity Lowell! Take the stand, please." They waited; no sign of her. They called her a second time, louder than before. I turned to look. The people in the back of the room were twisting their heads this way and that, but no one came forward. All the faces but one were unmistakably Caucasian—and that one belonged to the unforgetable Leroy, who was present again. She wasn't to have been a witness for the defense, far from it, but when it came down to it, Berenson's face showed more disappointment and worry than the prosecuting attorney's by far, I thought.

After a minute's hiatus, the case went grinding ponderously on without her. Westman called another name, one that I didn't recognize, and an unknown took the stand. The seemingly interminable succession of ebony witnesses had finally come to an end with him. Which was something. But even Leroy's sartorial splendor paled to nothingness compared to what was now on display. His clothes fitted as though they had been poured over him hot and allowed to harden. And he had a *gardenia* in his coat. Or maybe it was only a white carnation.

"Do you recognize this defendant?" said Westman ominously.

"I do," he said readily. "Like hell you do," I growled to myself, "when'd I ever see *you* before?"

"Tell the court your story," Westman ordered.

The new witness took hold of one cuff, and then the other, and meticulously pulled them down an inch below the sleeve of his coat. "The Saturday before I read about this murder," he announced in a clear, ringing voice that carried all the way to the end of the room and back with a lot left over, "I was coming out of the Cort Theater, where I worked at the time, and this man was standing at the stage entrance." Then all at once I remembered who he was. "Well, for the love of Mike!" I thought with a gasp, "is *that* going to be brought up too?" It wouldn't have surprised me any more to see my old teacher from school come parading in to tell all about how I had broken a window with an eraser in 8-B.

The stage-trained voice went on and on without even a moment's loss for a word, without even an "er" or an "um." For the first time since the trial had begun, I found myself a little uncomfortable, embarrassed, wishing I didn't have to sit there in the room. For all I knew, he might have every intention of telling *why* he had taken me up to the flat in the first place. But he had that part nicely under control, it soon appeared. "—when we got to where I lived, I found out that my friend the stage manager hadn't waited, he may have had a headache or something that evening, but the thing is he hadn't waited, he'd gone home. So I turned to this man and told him that *I* thought the best thing for him to do would be to call around at the theater the following Monday, a little earlier if possible to make sure my friend hadn't gone home yet, and *then* borrow the hundred dollars—never knowing what type person he was!" And he paused dramatically, with a neat little spread of the hands, to let my awful double-facedness sink in upon his listeners. "Before I quite realized what was happening," he went on, "he had forced his way in, struck me in the face so that I was simply *covered* with blood and nearly lost consciousness, and robbed *me* of the hundred dollars. *Me!*" he repeated with orchidaceous indignation, indicating his cravat, "who had tried to do him a good turn!" And flashing me a sulky look, as much as to say, "*Now* look what you got!" he turned his profile the other way.

I couldn't help noticing that the atmosphere in the court-room, particularly on the part of the spectators, wasn't nearly as sympathetic as it might have been, considering the amount of effort and dramatic suspense he had put into his recital. But it was reverence itself compared to what was brought on later, when Berenson had taken him over.

He began by asking him: "Did you report this incident to the police at the time it happened, Mr. Saint-Clair?"

"*Sin*clair. It's pronounced as if it were spelt s-i-n. I *told* Mr. Westman that."

Berenson roared, "I didn't ask you how you say your name! I asked you if you reported this alleged robbery to the police at the time!"

"No," replied the witness heatedly, "and you don't have to yell at me like that, either!"

When the gale of merriment had subsided and he could make himself audible once more, Berenson demanded, "Why not? Why didn't you?"

"For reasons of my own."

"Will you kindly tell the court what they are?" Berenson insisted.

"Because I was afraid it might hurt me professionally," Mr. Sinclair answered unwillingly. I could tell, even from where I was, that he was a little less at ease than he had been up to now.

"But you claim *you* were the one who was robbed," Berenson said dulcetly. "How could that hurt you professionally or otherwise?"

"Oh, I don't know," the witness answered peevishly. "I just had an idea that it might, that was all!"

I was almost expecting Berenson to wind up by getting him to admit *he* was the one who had done the robbing, before he was through.

"And yet you're willing enough to come here today and tell your story to the court, irrelevant as it may be. How is that, Mr. Sinclair?"

"I'm not working now," he said lamely. "I was then."

"Well, I don't pretend to understand the ethics of the theatrical profession," Berenson remarked stingingly. "We'll let that part of it go. Where did you have this money, this hundred and fifteen dollars you say the defendant stole from you?"

"In my apartment."

"We already know that, Mr. Sinclair," Berenson said patiently. "Just whereabouts was it? Under the rug?"

There was a preliminary titter or two from the back, but I, who already knew the answer that Berenson was bound to get if he kept on insisting, held on to the chair I was on.

The Sinclair gentleman suddenly lost the little temper that remained to him and blurted out vindictively, "In the bathroom, behind the toilet paper! *Now* are you satisfied?"

The judge had to threaten to have the room cleared no less than three times before the ribald outbursts this had brought on were effectively stemmed. It took nearly three minutes, I should judge. And by that time, the hunted yet venomous look on Mr. Sinclair's face would have drawn pity from any one but a courtroom audience.

When he was released from the stand (Berenson told me later that he cut such a ridiculous figure, he had benefited rather than harmed us), he made his way to the back of the room with a rapidity that almost resembled flight, and disappeared through the big frosted-glass doors to the accompaniment of a playful hiss from some young woman or other seated back there.

I thought he had come back again, possibly to avenge himself on her or on all of us, a moment later when I saw everyone's head turning that way, from the jury to the very court attendants, and heard a commotion at the door. People began to stand up in their seats here and there to look over the heads of others, and the judge's gavel had no effect for a moment or two. Westman hurriedly quit his place before the witness-box and disappeared toward the back of the room, and when a line of vision had been cleared, I saw him standing before a woman whose entire face was wound with bandages so that not even the eyes showed through, supported on either side by a colored man and woman as though she could hardly stand up.

She was taken out of the room again as soon as he had finished speaking to her two attendants, for it was evident that she herself couldn't talk, and after he had conferred with the judge, the latter rapped and announced that court was adjourned until the following day owing to the incapacitation of one of the principal witnesses for the state, Tenacity Lowell.

The way Berenson came to me when I had been escorted back, you would have thought his own life was at stake and not mine. "They threw acid at her," he gasped despondently, "right in the doorway of her own flat! She's lost an eye, and the whole lower part of her face's been eaten away—can't talk even if she wanted to." He gave me a searching look. "It's not going to be easy *now*, Wade."

"Do you think it has anything to do with this?" I asked him. "With the case?"

"Do I *think!*" he said bitterly.

"But she was Westman's witness—what would they want to bawl up the prosecution for like that, if I'm supposed to be taking the rap for some one?"

"Listen, you knew her when she was Pascal's maid—did she ever strike you as being anything intelligent? Well, whatever she knew, I could've gotten out of her. And she *knew,* all right! And they knew she knew. They weren't taking unnecessary chances—"

"Gee, that was a lousy thing to do," I commented.

"Feel sorry for yourself, Wade," he advised me knowingly. "If it wasn't for that very wench there, Pascal would be alive right now in California with you. She was the one sent them the tip-off that night—I know what I'm talking about!" He lit a cigarette and shook it at me when it was lit. "She got Pascal *hers* that night. And now, indirectly, she's getting you yours. Don't look at me like that," he said fiercely. "Do you think I'm talking through my hat or something! I had a damn good chance of getting you out of it if Westman had put her on the stand. And now—you may as well hear it from me as from any one else—I think it's too late for me to pull you through. You're in the soup."

"And what about it?" I said. "I could've been in Montreal or Winnipeg the day after it happened, if I'd wanted to. And *still* be there today, if I'd wanted to badly enough. Only I didn't want to. I wanted to be where I am. And I wanted to get just what I'm *going* to get, nothing less and nothing more."

"The case is closing," he warned me, "and there's not much time left! There's only one thing that might still do some good— how much I don't know. I can let you take the stand yourself— in your own defense."

"Do that," I said, "and hear all about how I choked Bernice Pascal to death."

"You're insane," he spat at me. "I should have pleaded that for you in the first place."

"Sane or insane," I told him grimly, "cook I must—in the big, high chair."

"Don't bother wishing for it," he said. "It'll come quickly enough. And once this case closes, Mr. Know-it-all, an appeal isn't going to help any!" He flung his cigarette down, reached over, and caught me by the wrist. "Get up there, will you, Wade, if I call on you tomorrow, and tell them the truth—for the love of Christ, tell them the truth! Tell them how you loved her—tell them what she meant to you—talk to them just like you have to me at times—*they're* not morons, *they'll* understand how it is you couldn't have possibly done it. My God, there's something sincere about you when you start talking about her—that would get *any*one! Any one who was ever young, who was ever in love himself—" With his hand glued to my wrist, he kept shaking me by the arm. "What can I say to you, fellow, to make you understand? *Tell* them how she auctioned herself off for a hundred dollars that night—*tell them,* don't be ashamed! *Tell* them how you went out hunting it up. *Tell* them how you robbed this actor. It's not going to hurt you; it's going to help you, if anything! You did it for *her.* You'll have that jury in the hollow of your hand. The average man is more of a sentimentalist deep down in himself than any woman alive. Why, the very fact that you signed that confession may be all to the good in the end! You loved her so—that you didn't want to live; that stands to reason. *I* still have the taxi driver, to tell them how you were all the way down to Grand Central, could have gotten away beautifully! How're they going to get around the fact that you didn't even know how she had been killed when you first told your story to the police? *I'll* take care of that, *I'll* bring it all out when I sum up—but you—you've *got* to get up there and help me! We've still got this one chance, Wade, slim as it is—don't be a quitter, you owe me something; do this much for me at least. Other clients plead with their lawyers to get them out; here's a lawyer pleading with his client—"

"If you want me to take the stand," I said wearily, "I'll take the stand. But when Westman asks me if I killed her, and he will, I'm going to say yes. That's all I've got left now, the determination to die. I'm going to hang on to it."

I heard him swearing at me then; making all kinds of noise. I almost thought he was going to hit me in the jaw, he was so furious. I'm positive he would have liked to. I simply didn't listen, shut all the crannies of my mind and didn't hear him. Then, after a while, he was gone, and I was by myself again. Glad of it, too. I did what I did every other night—ate my meal when it was brought in to me, and then took a cigarette out of the flattened, crumpled pack I kept in my back pocket, that the turnkey used to buy for me two or three times a week. I gave him a quarter each time—fifteen cents for the thirteen-cent package and ten cents for himself for doing me the favor of getting it. When I was through smoking it, I took off my coat and vest and shoes and pants and went to sleep on the cot in my shirt, tie, socks, and underwear. I didn't bother taking my tie off ever, because I had a good, even knot in it (from the time I'd first come in here) and I didn't imagine there was much chance of getting it that accurate a second time without a mirror or anything. Not that it would have mattered, but I was tired of tying neckties around myself all my life long, like I was of everything else.

The next day in court, Berenson had me take the stand— maybe to call my bluff, or maybe because there was nothing else left for him to do any more. He gave me a long, long look, and then he said in a low voice, "Tell your story, Wade," and then he didn't look at me any more but just sat there looking down at the floor. I couldn't even tell if he was listening or not.

I told it briefly, I wanted to get it over with; began abruptly at what had been practically the end of it.

"We were going to California. She wanted to go to California because it was far from New York, and she didn't like New York any more. I bought the tickets and went home and packed my valise—" At this point, I saw Maxine sitting at the back of the room, the very end seat, on the aisle. "Poor kid," I thought remorsefully, "just today she had to come here! I told him to tell her to stay away." Her face was just like a little round white golfball at that distance. "So small an area," I thought, "to suffer so much."

"When I got there, the doorman insisted he hadn't called me up and given me any message. I went upstairs anyway, and found her there—"

I stopped a minute, with stage fright or something. If Berenson had shut up, maybe I would have told it the way he wanted me to, the way it had—I suppose—really been.

"Alive or dead?" he said, without looking up from the floor.

"Alive," I said.

He didn't bat an eyelash, although for him it probably meant five or ten thousand a year income from now on instead of fifty or seventy-five or a hundred.

Maxine didn't move, either. I could still see her way over there in the corner, but there was something whiter than her face now in front of it—a handkerchief, I suppose.

"She told me she wasn't going with me after all. I asked her why. She said I didn't have enough money. I caught hold of her by the neck, and after awhile we both fell to the floor and she was dead. I went downstairs without any one seeing me and got into a taxi. Then I came back again—"

"Your defendant," Berenson said dismally, the minute I had stopped speaking.

"You admit you killed her, Mr. Wade?" Westman said as soon as he stood up. The "Mr. Wade" was my reward, I guess, for being the admirable defendant I was.

"I'm no doctor, Mr. Prosecuting Attorney," I said. "I choked her, and she didn't move any more. I guess she died then."

"Would you like us to believe," he sneered, "that you didn't intend her to die? That the strangulation was unpremeditated?"

Something blew up inside me, and I sprang to my feet with smarting eyes that blurred out all the faces before me. "You don't think I *wanted* to kill her, do you!" I shouted in the direction I'd last seen his face a moment ago. "That much I'll never admit! How could I want to kill her, damn you, when she was the only thing I had!" And I flopped back in the chair again and brushed my sleeve across my face.

A few minutes later I was out of the box, back where I always sat. I can't remember if he asked me any more questions after that or not. The deepening fog that had begun to settle over me from that point on didn't lift any more. All I knew was, she was gone! gone! *gone!* Why did they keep this up, months afterward, week in and week out? Why didn't they let *me* go too!

Maxine came up to me for a minute when I was being led out that day. "Don't you realize what you've done?" I forced my mind to come back to where I was standing, looking at her. "Wade, if they do this thing to you, I want to go too."

I felt my mouth smiling the way I told it to, and said to her: "Isn't one of us being here better than none of us being here?"

And I was even going to reach out and touch her on the face to try to make her feel better, but while I was thinking about it, she and the courtroom moved slowly away and I discovered I was back in the cell again holding a thick mug of milk and coffee to my mouth. So I knew I couldn't do it any more because she was no longer with me.

The next day, I think it was, they both summed up their cases—Westman and Berenson—so I knew it must at last be about over. Oh, God, I was sick of having loved her, of having killed her or not killed her, of having known her at all! I wanted the nothingness that was coming to come even quicker—when there would be no Bernice, no Wade, no New York.

Right after those thirteen that had been there all along went out, I was taken out too. And when I was brought in again, they filed in too. And when the one on the end stood up, I cared less than any one in the room what he was going to say. Then the word "Guilty" came floating toward me like a golden balloon in the air, the reward for all I had been through.

And it grew dark, and it grew light again, and it grew dark and light again. Maybe six times, or maybe sixteen times or maybe sixty. And they kept bringing me back to that place, and bringing me back to that place, and bringing me back to that place. And the last time they brought me back, the judge spoke for a long time, and ended up by saying, "and may God have mercy on your soul." Then I heard a loud cry in a corner of the room, and turned that way, and saw Maxine lying on the floor. And while the world rolled on without her, I wondered if she had died then or was still living. But some day soon, soon now, the world won't have to wonder that about me.